Orphalina

About *Orphalina* (*Árvácska* , 1941)

Arguably the most gut-wrenching, and simul-taneously the most lyrical of Zsigmond Móricz's numerous novels, *Orphalina* recounts events inspired by the real-life experiences of Erzsébet Litkei (1916-1971), an orphaned girl whom Móricz met in Budapest in 1934. As the tragic fate of "Orphalina State," the protagonist in this novel, reveals, Litkei was clearly a touchstone for Móricz in his quest to reveal the deepest layers of suffering in interwar Hungarian society, and to uncover the forces at work in stifling the agency of human beings deserving of access to a good life.

Orphalina

Written as *Árvácska* in 1941 by Zsigmond
Móricz
Translated from the Hungarian by
Virginia L. Lewis

Nem sűlyed az emberiség!

Ilyen gonosz vala rég,

Ilyen gonosz már kezdet óta ...

Hisz különben nem kellett vóna

Százféle mesét,

Eget, isteneket,

Pokolt és ördögöket

Gondolni ki, hogy zaboláztassék.

- Sándor Petőfi

Contents

Introduction   9

First Psalm   17

Second Psalm   45

Third Psalm   61

Fourth Psalm   89

Fifth Psalm   121

Sixth Psalm   139

Seventh Psalm   199

About the Translator   257

Introduction

Orphalina (1941) was one of the last novels written by Hungarian author Zsigmond Móricz (1879-1942). Originally titled *Árvácska*, meaning "little orphan" (*árvácska* also has the botanical meaning of "pansy"), the work was inspired by the childhood experiences of Erzsébet Litkei (1916-1971), a foundling whom Móricz met in 1934 when Litkei was eighteen years old, the daughter of an unknown father and a suicidal mother. Although thirty-seven years her senior, Móricz grew so close to Litkei that she became not only his muse, but also his lover – their mutual child, Imre, was born in April 1935. Because Móricz was married at the time, the true nature of his relationship to Litkei, whom he called "Csibe," was not public, and Móricz in fact ultimately legally adopted Csibe, along with young Imre.

Csibe's experiences growing up as an impoverished orphan in rural Hungary, as well as the trials she experienced upon escaping to Budapest as a teenager, proved a rich source of inspiration for

Móricz in the years leading up to the writing of *Árvácska*, arguably his most gut-wrenching and at the same time most lyrical novel – from 1936-37 Móricz produced twenty-eight novellas based on Litkei's stories, in addition to some fifteen hundred pages of notes. Erzsébet Litkei was clearly a touchstone for Móricz in his quest to reveal the deepest layers of suffering in interwar Hungarian society, and to uncover the forces at work in stifling the agency of human beings deserving of access to a good life. Her nickname means "chick" and alludes effectively to the sweet fragility and tender innocence of a little child cast like flotsam into the arms of a hostile society – there are numerous plays on Csibe's name in *Orphalina*, beginning with the protagonist's nickname "Csöre," a term used to call chicks in Hungarian and thus rendered as "Chick-Chick" in this translation, and proceeding to plays on the "cs" (/tʃ/, English "ch") consonant with which her name begins. The author's Pygmalion-like relationship with Csibe lends proof to the capacity of love and compassion for fostering flourishing and positive human development. After Móricz died in September, 1942, Csibe married Dr. Károly Keresztes, a lawyer and literary advocate, and together they established a publishing house in Zsigmond Móricz's name, using their resources there not only to publish worthy works of Hungarian literature, but also to rescue Jews from deportation and murder. Erzsébet Móricz-Keresztes was recognized posthumously for these efforts, along with her husband, in 1996 by Yad Vashem. As for Imre Móricz, he earned his doctorate and became a mechanical engineer.

The skills evinced by the author in developing the raw material offered him by his muse to create the short novel *Orphalina* reveal Zsigmond Móricz in his full creative maturity. *Orphalina* was in fact not especially well received when it was first published – as Zsófia Szilágyi argues, the work was quite simply ahead of its time: this was due in part to the readership's fear of somehow sharing in responsibility for the fate of the human beings symbolized by the novel's main character, and in part to Móricz's disruption of traditional literary forms.[1] For clearly Móricz aims to draw readers into Orphalina's suffering in a way that pushes them to confront society's shared culpability in creating her

---

[1] Zsófia Szilágyi, "Mélységek és nyomjelek: Nádas Péter és Móricz Zsigmond," in: *Alföld*, vol. 58, no. 12, Dec. 2007.

misery. Likewise his division of the book into "psalms" rather than chapters, and his portrayal of the abused and exploited orphan's life journey as what resembles stations of the cross, represented an alienating approach to narrative structure, particularly during World War II when calming escapism was sought after over raw naturalism. By contrast, the alienating aspects of Orphalina's story, alongside the innovative use of multiple narrative perspectives and provocative manipulation of biblical and mythic allusions,[2] appeal to modern readers, who seek out opportunities to gain meaningful insights into the tendency of contemporary societal and economic forces to reduce their agency and strip people of their humanity. This explains the keen interest elicited by the text in recent years, and also occasions the writing of this first translation of *Árvácska* into English.

Any great work of literature poses challenges to the individual who dares to translate it into a new language, and *Orphalina* is no exception. Móricz mines his native Hungarian for every opportunity to

---

[2] Takács Miklós, "Ió lánya: Nemek, átváltozások, a szöveg idegensége és az idegen 'szövegesedése' Móricz Zsigmond *Árvácskájában*," in: *Irodalomtörténet* 2003/9.

realize the unique perspectives of the work's characters on the events that unfold there. Thus Orphalina's first foster mother, who shares to a poignant extent in the sufferings that characterize the orphan's young life, vents her perpetual disillusionment in a language marked largely by the curses and exclamations peculiar to the Hungarian plains in the 1920s. The language used by the old weaver, the one human being who makes Orphalina's years with her second foster family bearable, is marked by a unique mixture of deference and defiance grown out of his experience as a man who was both a responsible agent and an oppressed victim as a member of the rural working class. The third and last family on Orphalina's journey through suffering is of Swabian-German descent and injects their stiff Hungarian with German terms the little girl only comes to understand as they are used to intensify her oppression. And Orphalina herself is present behind much of the narrative writing in the novel: her naïve and uneducated nature informs especially those passages that most directly recount the abuse she suffers. Móricz pushes the limits of literary expression by making the little girl's speech unintelligible when she attempts to communicate through language the more traumatic aspects of her experiences. What her second foster family in particular ridicules as the girl's inherent lack of capacity for proper speech is in fact a direct result of the external forces thrust upon her that make of her a victim of society's objectification of even its most innocent members. Her "lisping" is thus a symptom not of Orphalina's presumed inadequacy, but rather a manifestation and condemnation of society's own inadequacy, namely its capacity for reducing human beings to abject objects.

In attempting to realize Móricz's *Árvácska* as an English-language text, I have made every effort to retain the author's intentions in the use of his native language as intactly as reasonably possible. Without a doubt the result may strike readers as stretching somewhat the expressive capacity of the English language. Given the fact that Móricz sought to provoke his readers into sensing with at least some degree of authenticity the alienating nature of his protagonist's life experiences, this result may be deemed an asset. Of course no translation, no matter how skillful, can ever replace the original text. But in a case such as this where an important work of literature is composed in a language that is accessible to only a limited readership, the attempt to realize it in English, a language that is used by a far greater population, is warranted. It is my hope that my effort to retain to the greatest extent possible the author's original style, his symbolism, his voice, his allusions, even his punctuation, will allow readers of this translation to experience as authentically as feasible the world both sacred and profane that he created around his troubled protagonist, "Orphalina State."

Virginia L. Lewis, Northern State University

First Psalm

Dawn breaks on the puszta.

The harsh, relentless sun nudges upward where the sky's edge meets the earth, like the underdeveloped egg of an ungainly chicken. Red and yellow rays crackle forth into the blue fog of dawn. The egg still lacks a shell, the sun stretches out uncertainly, as though melting apart; the egg breaks across the brown frying pan of earth.

A small farmstead on the endless puszta.

A small house from out of a fairy tale, with its blackened thatched roof, dark with moss, its crown battered by stork and storm, looking in spite of its thick cob walls for all the world like a puffball, ready to fall in one day on its occupants, but that is still a ways off, during some storm in a yet distant winter's night.

Today it's still a happy farmstead. Here everything can only be pretty, can only be good and content. The ancient dwelling place of human creatures. No fence in sight, not a trace; what would be the point? The next closest farmstead lies a pathless eternity from here. Not even the poultry needs fencing. Nothing worth scratching up here – when the hens flutter down from the two bent mulberry trees, they go straight to the neighboring stubblefield to scratch about.

How nice it would be to live here, to rest here. How nice to be a child here.

A little child does indeed stand in the field, a diminutive wisp of a girl, beneath the immense sky, rubbing the sleep from her eyes with her two little fists, she stands there as God created her, naked beneath the upward gaze of the sun.

The birds are just waking up and immediately begin their cheerful chirping, while the little human chick stands there sulking, stands and sulks. A tiny, thin, brown body, like some small animal, covered in dew.

Not a thought occupies her mind, she doesn't even know how she came to be out here. Sleepy. Like a kitten, but this knows better how to purr and wash, the child just stands there, just stands without hope, or is there hope in the little heath flower that stands in the dawn and trembles its way open beneath the sun?

❀

A drawn, haggard woman steps out into the yard. Poof, the sun has risen, two spans high, and it's already a glowing white orb, better not look at it.

The woman looks as though she's swallowed the largest melon in the field whole, her apron hangs so oddly, is she hiding it there? Did she steal the melon? Six children wriggle through the dwarfish door into the fresh air, the good mother looks after all of them at once, her immediate concern consisting in calling after them with her tired, whining voice to impart the moral lesson: "The devil take your sorry hides!"

The sun has no other task than to measure in spans what the people are doing on the earth.

Peering already out over the thatched roof, it sees that the two big boys are carrying a haversack around their necks, that's where their food is. They're headed for the grape vines with their father, that grouchy man with the bloodshot eyes, who's shuffling about there around the animals. There's work to be done at the farmstead – where there are animals, there's always work. The animals need plants, the plants need the hoe, and the hoe needs men. That's why the farmstead is happy, because someone is always occupying himself with it from morning till night, whoever wants work will find it on the farm; whoever has work has bread, has wine, has good humor, is happy.

The younger four children are headed to school. Four of them still go to school. The smallest one too, to whom the mother is now giving a shirt – little Rózsi dons it proudly, it's of good, strong linen, and on the shoulder is a stamp, a stamp as big as a child's hand, with letters circling round the edge. The good mother looks at her littlest one in the new shirt. The mother doesn't feel like talking at this early hour, she just looks at her, not even telling her to be careful with it. She's pleased that her daughter has a new shirt; all four of them are dressed now, they can go. The day is still dawning, but they should get on their way, they have to go four and a half kilometers across the puszta to reach the school, they're obligated to go, because if they don't, their parents will be punished. And how lovely it is in any case, the farmstead teeming with life, chickens scratching among the buttonweed, little black guineafowl always crowding together, all of them wanting to pick at one and the same kernel, ducks and geese honking, back a ways the cow is mooing, and little Rózsi is heading off to the distant school in her new shirt. But off to the back, behind the yard, the seventh child creeps forth, the naked one, the state one, because the good mother keeps, alongside the chickens and the piglets, a state child for her own use, for whom the state pays her eight pengős per month, and every spring and fall she receives a shirt, a pair of socks, and a jacket, and for the winter a sturdy woolen shawl; they even give her a pair of children's boots. How nice that is for her own children in this difficult world where everything is so dear. All of good quality, very much to be prized: "Don't you go tearing that shirt, you!" It's not a lot, that's true, the lady of the manor is supposed to give them two of everything, two shirts, two pairs of socks, two jackets, but she only gives them one, lord knows what she does with the others, no doubt she gives them to him who gives something to her in return. But let a person just say one word of complaint, and she shoots back: "Don't lie, they were both there." And for good measure she adds: "Say too much and I'll take the child away from you ..." So the good mother acquiesces, because it's true, it would be nice to have two of each garment, but having what she gets is nice, too. Where there are lots of children, every little bit is appreciated.

The unclothed state child watches the bustling preparations for a bit, then she speaks up:

"That's my shirt. Mama dear, that's my shirt. Mama dear is putting my shirt on Rózsi."

"Do you wanna pipe down? Just look at her, coming back here instead of getting to work, the little pig. Where are the turnip greens? You wanna just shut up?"

The schoolbound children snigger as they watch the little child from the state standing there naked before the porch, her contorted face staring toward the shirt which she can no longer see, because Rózsi has already drawn the little jacket over it. She doesn't recognize the jacket, she's still too small to wear that, but she recognized the shirt, heaven knows how, maybe because of the stamp, but who clued her in on the fact that the stamp was from the Orphanage – it still couldn't be washed out enough.

The children get milk from the bucket, for this the cow stands leisurely alone there in the yard, she'll be milked momentarily by the melon-bellied woman, on the very turnip greens the state orphan fetched from the turnip field behind the house. There in the bucket is the milk. Each child holds his cup out and gets some milk, and they all slurp greedily, downing the raw, unfiltered liquid. They love the milk.

Only that rotten state child doesn't like it. This insufferable gourmand, I've no idea what she'll eat, what to cook up for her.

"Get your cup!"

But the state child maintains her hostile silence, training a covetous eye on the shirt Rózsi is wearing. No one knows why the milk disgusts her so. The others laugh at her and how stupid she is not to like the nice fresh milk, no matter how they prod her, she refuses it, they hold the milk jug under her nose, she throws up, it's hilarious.

"She's after Rózsi's shirt," the biggest girl says with a knowing wink, like one who is in on the theft, how they steal the shirt from off the little state girl's body, because she's not a sibling like they are, she's just a state sibling.

"Watch it!" the good mother shrieks; she beats her daughter, angry over her revealing that she sees through the deception, and in the meantime the wretched girl has spilled milk on her own jacket. The poor mother loses her patience over this, she yells at her own flesh and blood as furiously as though the girl had sought to murder her father and mother:

"Can't you be careful, you filthy brat! Can't you just be careful! I should just up and break your neck!"

But in truth she's only yelling like this to put the fear of God in the state child, so that it won't occur to her to dare utter another word, as unpredictable as she is – truth is, she's mortally afraid the little state child might mention the stamped shirt yet again. Besides, what does she even need it for? Is she going to freeze now, in the middle of summer? When could she have grown so accustomed to it, since she never goes about with a shirt or any clothing on: she's just fine like this, the unwanted thing, abandoned by her mother; as little as she is and already she's developed a sense of greed, believing that something actually belongs to her!

She promptly stirs the slop for the piglets, with a little bran mixed in – this too she does more as though she were stealing the bran from them rather than giving it to them, for when a person is raising a piglet, she has to give it bran, but it's expensive and hard to come by, so she just sprinkles it on top like salt.

"Chick-Chick."

That's what she calls her, that's the little nameless girl's name, somehow it's stuck with her: "Chick-Chick!" they call the state orphan, "Chick-Chick!"

The little girl is still standing there pouting – does it still bother her about the shirt? How sensitive she is. How she stares, the little assassin.

"How long are you gonna loaf around, you? Are you taking Borisa out to graze?"

The little loner, whose every thought went off to school with the children, for she too would like to be big, so that she could go the long, long way across the fields, far, far off to school with her siblings. In a new shirt, a nice jacket, with a nice new kerchief, her bread for school wrapped inside – she's already just as big as Rózsi too, and yet she's left here. Maybe if they put her shirt on her … but she'd still prefer to go as she is, if she could. Because she doesn't know what it means that the shirt belongs to her, yet it still hurts her that they gave it to Rózsi, and she just stands there and picks her nose.

The mother went inside for a bit of bran, in the end she felt badly for the piglets; with her bran-covered hands she cuts a piece of bread: she started off with a bigger piece, but as she cut the knife thought better and took it upon itself to cut a smaller piece.

"So, here's your bread. But don't eat it right away, otherwise you can just stay hungry till noon."

The little girl took the bread and just stood there.

"There's your switch. Off with you. Borisa wants to graze already. But don't just wander about, follow the wagon track. You know our fields? You're not so dumb that you don't know them by now. You know them?"

The child said nothing, she still held her head down, and now she looked at the little piece of bread in her hand; she formed a pout with her small mouth, looked at the little piece of bread, which wasn't really that small, but wasn't big either, it was just bread, a thick little chunk, and as she looked at it, she began to grow very hungry for it, but she wouldn't bite into it, as she had to consume it slowly, at Bori's side, while Bori was grazing. The cow.

"Borisa, don't … no, not there …"

The little girl held a switch in her hand, a switch whose end was divided into three strips, with this she struck the cow, the cow loped along, and she ran after her, striking her with the switch.

Her eyes were brimming with tears, but she had no idea why, from what?

She was barely able to make out the path. Tall grass was growing there that no one ever mowed. The grass on the path is mowed by wagon wheels and hoed by animals' hooves. But few farm carts travel here. Only those belonging to nearby landowners. Last week István Mágócs came this way, yes indeed, and he stopped while she was minding the cow, and laughed as he saw how the girl stood naked by the cow's tail. He tried to lure her as well, as he always said a word or two to her, but she ran away. He doesn't know why she ran off, it was just something she did when she saw a stranger. It was a habit with her, like a pup who runs from whatever it doesn't know. It could also be that she runs because she has no clothes on, he couldn't say for sure if that were the case. Not that she's unaccustomed to it, it's just that others sometimes make fun of her, call her nakey, gypsy girl, dirty jaybird, although a person would have to be a fool to find that surprising, after all she never had any clothes, not even a shirt, only in winter, when it was freezing cold and she had to go outdoors, then they gave her the rags cast off by the other children. But these were never to her liking, they were foul-smelling rags and she was ashamed to wear them.

But now there was little chance of avoiding an encounter, as the cow was headed towards Kadarcs's cart, which was loaded with corn fodder and already headed home at this early hour with the feed for his cattle.

Chick-Chick ran barefoot into the large stubblefield that was already overgrown with thyme and other wild herbs. The stubble was no longer so prickly since it had rained several times and the wheat stems had already begun to rot where the scythe had cut them off.

"Come 'ere, Chick-Chick, come on over here, you little chicken."

Chick-Chick didn't answer but ran off, then laughed and looked back at István Kadarcs, who likewise laughed and winked at her. "I'm gonna go out once more, then I'll bring you a little bread with honey, all right?"

The little girl looked at him with wide eyes. She really didn't know what bread with honey was, nevertheless her mouth watered at the thought of all that sweetness. She still had her own day's piece of bread. She held it and guarded it doggedly, she wouldn't have bitten into it for the world. The bread was salted, too, she really liked it when salt was sprinkled on it, plus it was a little smeared, because Mama dear still had bran on her hands when she'd sliced it.

"Chase her off!" she yelled at István Kadarcs. "Chase her off ... Chase her oofff ..."

"The cow?"

"Chase her ooffff ..."

Like the birds of the puszta, the little girl said only a few words, which she repeated over and over again ... She didn't know how to speak properly yet, for who was there to speak with ... At home she wasn't allowed to – the other children had permission to scold her, but she must always keep silent, because if she speaks, the consequences are painful and swift ...

"Git ..." István Kadarcs said, and he struck the cow's behind with the whip, all the more eagerly as it began tearing into the fodder corn on the wagon.

The cow raised her back end in the air and kicked out behind her. She wasn't accustomed to being whipped, as the little girl's strokes don't smart, they only caress. And she loves little Chick-Chick, she always recognizes the child when she takes her out to graze.

She began to make circles across the field, as she knew that this land belonged to them, here she could graze day in and day out and duke it out with the flies.

István Kadarcs said nothing more to the little girl. He saw that he would have to run a long ways after her if he wanted to catch her. A bit later, in the afternoon heat, the child would be worn out ...

Chick-Chick had already forgotten that her eyes were trained on the wagon, she was really only looking in the direction where it was headed. She was looking toward the village where the children had gone to school. The village was so far away that even the church tower wasn't visible. In the distance it was so tiny that the trees hid it from her view.

It was never clear to her what she saw in that direction. She kept looking there as though expecting something in particular, but the fact was that the little wild girl expected nothing from anywhere at all.

"Borisa, don't ... not there, you ..."

Borisa, having made a large arc around her, was just returning to her, and Chick-Chick wanted to send the cow back in the other direction, since in her mind her purpose in accompanying Borisa was to tell the beast to go over there when she was here, and to come here when she was over there ...

"Borisa, don't ..."

The cow seems to want to rub her head against her, nudging the child from below with her big wet nose, rooting around in her hand, and before the girl can manage to tell the cow no, not there, she wraps her long tongue around the dense, salty bread in her hand and swallows it.

"Borisa, don't ..."

By this time she's lying on the ground, as the silly cow has knocked her down as though in play, seeming in her own way to laugh at the child while eating her bread.

"Not there, youu ... oouu ..."

Tears flow down her cheeks. The silly beast is gorging herself on her bread, crumbs smeared along her wet lips, then a chunk of bread slides off ... drops onto the ground ...

The splendid field. Gigantic wheatfields surrounding the farm, only God knows whose they are, everything from here to the distant reeds, all splendid fields. Beautiful bloom-covered fields. Tiny flowers blossomed there. Scented flowers. The girl was as close to the flowers as a little bee and sniffed the lovely scents.

A stake had been driven into the ground.

Everywhere there were stakes. That's where they tied the cow, but Chick-Chick didn't know how to do that, only the big kids tied the cow up if they came.

They also drove Borisa out with a club, another reason why Borisa liked little Chick-Chick, because she urged Borisa out with a switch, and Borisa was already telling herself, oh, how nice, today will be another nice day, little Chick-Chick is taking me out with the switch, not those clubbers. That's why she was making circles, and she even got the salty, branny bread out of Chick-Chick's little hand.

And there was a nice nut tree there too, a tall nut tree, its branches reached all around down to the ground; no one saw when someone was sitting under this tree.

And the old haystack was also there, far away. She didn't like going over there, as the corn is out that way, and whenever papa dear was out there hoeing the corn, he always had to take her along, and he took her on his old felt peasant's coat.

That's why she didn't even like looking over there.

Bori was heading into the grape vines.

Oh no, the grape vines.

The grape vines – that's where Bori had gone to. Little Borisa. In the grape vines.

Right, while Chick-Chick was gaping off elsewhere, and crying over her bread, and being angry at Borisa. And the cow has trampled a grape vine. It's nothing a cow even needs. She just tramples it.

Oh my, that stirred up a ruckus. All day long no one notices the cow, or even her, not even when the cow eats all her bread, but they saw it right away when the cow trampled a grape vine. Papa dear gave her a serious tongue-lashing.

"Just wait, you wretch, that's what you eat my bread for. There'll be no supper for you."

But she dared to answer back: "Don't want any."

All day long, whenever they saw her, they scolded her because the cow had broken the grape vine. But they turned a deaf ear over Borisa's having eaten her bread.

"No supper for you!"

"Don't want any."

But she hadn't gotten any lunch either. Mama dear had been so angry with her that she hadn't brought her anything to eat.

In the evening she sat on the floor with the children, and mama dear pushed a plate of food towards her as well.

"Eat."

But Chick-Chick just sat there pouting. Mama dear had long since forgotten her, only she saw the food still resting there on the floor.

"Why aren't you eating? Eat that, now."

"Don't want to."

They were stunned.

"You said I wouldn't get my dinner – I'm not gonna eat yours!"

"Chick-Chick, Chick-Chick, to hell with you."

"Tohellwithyou, I'm just tohellwithyou."

The gaunt, sickly woman, her mama dear, gawked at her: "What are you muttering there, you ninny! Is that how you treat your mother who raises you and feeds you? Come here this instant."

The little girl went to her, slowly, lurkingly, suspiciously – she knew exactly what was coming. She held her two little hands behind her, over her buttocks.

When she'd gotten close enough, mama dear grabbed her arm, pulled her towards her, then put her across her knee and thrashed her until her weak arm gave out.

Gasping, she finally let up. "Now kiss my hand."

The girl lowered her head defiantly.

"Kiss my hand when I tell you to. I'll slice you in half. You're gonna disrespect me? You'd better apologize ..."

The girl mumbled an apology, but only she and mama dear knew what she said.

"Now give me your paw."

She held out her hand and the girl had to take it, then she turned it over and the child had to press a kiss onto her grimy, black, veiny hand.

Once she'd done this as propriety demanded, the mother yelled as though suddenly recalling something urgent:

"Go, run and fetch some corn from the loft."

The child ran off cheerfully, forgetting everything but her errand. In order to reach the loft, she had to climb up from the manger in the stable, as in place of the ladder the dung-barrow was leaning against the loft, and it was very difficult to climb up that. But when she started back with the basket, she fell head over heels into the hay. She didn't hurt herself, but all the corn spilled out of the basket, and she screamed her head off.

"Don't scream, they'll think I'm doing you in! Come here!"

The little girl climbed out of the manger, her cries turning to whimpers, and went over to her. Mrs. Dudás gave her a few taps on the back and a light slap on the head.

"You can go."

Then she noticed that the corn had spilled out into the hay, so now she had to climb into the loft herself and gather up the ears.

She groaned, she cursed, no longer did she fear that people might think she was doing the child in: she was doing her in.

Once, a week or so later, she herself was up in the loft, and when she was climbing back down, the dung-barrow slipped out from under her and she fell into the manger such that her skirt got hung up above her and she just dangled there naked.

Chick-Chick shrieked with laughter, dancing:

"Look at that, mama dear, when I fell there, I got slapped, but you spilled the corn, too."

"To hell with you, you wretch. Laughing at me ..." Once she'd extracted herself from the manger, she gathered her strength so she could give the child a proper thrashing. "Wanna laugh at me again? Gonna do it again? You'd better apologize. Say after me: 'I apologize to mama dear for my bad behavior, I'll never misbehave again.' Now give me your paw, so I have your hand on it that you'll never be naughty again ... So, how's it gonna be?" She used her outstretched hand to slap the child's face and then held it out again for her to kiss. "You gonna kiss my hand now?"

Little Chick-Chick kissed the grubby, vein-covered hand, these bulging veins, then she said:

"I'd rather go out to the field with Borisa, 'cause Borisa doesn't hit me, but you hit."

"Devil's spawn, you chicken from Pest. So little, yet poisonous as a snake."

"I'm not a chicken from Pest," Chick-Chick said, stomping her feet, "then Rozi must be a chicken from Pest too, but mama dear never calls Rozi a chicken from Pest, only I'm a chicken from Pest. I'm gonna go into the round lake and let a snake eat me, then you can cry over me."

"Let the devil cry over you," mama dear grumbled, and she went inside with the corn which she'd gathered up in the meantime, all the while bickering with the child through the slats about chicken from Pest here, chicken from Pest there.

And there was the round lake, large, large, very large, and it really was round and truly a lake.

Next to it were the reeds, that's where the snake lived. No one was allowed to bathe there, since the snake came out in the summer, and it nabbed a child's leg; little Chick-Chick doesn't know what became of the leg, either, whether the snake ate it or not.

That's how it was with the reeds, and that's where they used to go with mama dear, as that's where the corn was, and that's where the melons were.

"You can't go there, my child," mama dear said, "the snake will eat you."

So when little Chick-Chick tended the cow here, she didn't go off toward the reeds, she went off to the melons. And there she saw a pretty melon, and she picked it, but she didn't have a knife and couldn't cut it up, but she didn't go hungry there with her food in front of her, no, she grasped the melon, hurled it good onto the ground, the melon broke apart, and now she could dig into its innards, with her hands she extracted the nice red insides, and she made a wondrous meal of it. But Bori was happy too, as she gave the cow the rind, and Borisa nibbled it so clean that, when mama dear came, little Chick-Chick praised her for doing such nice work of eating the flesh from the melon.

"Where did you get the melon from?"

"I found it on the ground."

"Is it all right to pick melons? You wretch, is it allowed to pick melons off the ground? Don't you know, you miserable pig, that we have to sell the melons, and you dare go and pick them? Is it your melon? Am I raising you to be a thief? You're gonna become a thief on me?"

And then came the beating.

The little girl didn't understand it, they would always pick these melons when they wanted to eat them. Papa dear picked them, mama dear picked them, even the children did it. They had to knock on the melons one after the other, and pick the ones that had a nice clean sound. Now she had no idea why she was being beaten. So far no one else got beaten, only her.

"But why am I wearing myself out like this," mama dear said, "come on home, papa dear can do it."

The little girl didn't believe mama dear would snitch on her to papa dear. For it wasn't only the children who feared him, she did as well. For the father beat no one more than his wife. With his stick, with his club he lit into the small, gaunt woman! And if she ran away, he slung his club after her like the cowherd did after the cow, and struck her, causing mama dear to fall to the ground, and the man assailed her and kicked her right and left, he even trampled her. And now mama dear would snitch on her to the father? She didn't believe that for a moment, nonetheless she went home in fear with the cow that evening. They milked the cow, her udder bulged like a frightfully large bag from between her two back legs, like a filled sack, from the corners of which flowed the fatty milk, and when papa dear came, his wife was perhaps afraid that her number was up again, but she said to him:

"So, so, just keep an eye out once, Dudás, she stole! She went to the melon field and picked the prettiest melon, which we could've sold."

Maybe she said that so that, if the man went out to the field and didn't find the melon, he wouldn't come after her with his stick, but the little girl quickly saw how the father's features contorted themselves, and never had father Dudás looked at her that way, he who had always hugged her and petted her, and said it wasn't allowed to tell that to their mother, and she didn't tell it, but mother nonetheless tattled on her to their father.

Their father was just looking for the ember to light his pipe with when his wife told him that. In no time he was bellowing, louder than Borisa. His mouth was opened so wide that his red moustache hairs stood out like bristles.

"She stole? Stooooole? This piece of shit stole a melon? ... Come here, you won't be stealing anymore ... even if it bites you on the hand, you won't be stealing anything more. Just close the door so she can't get out."

The children rushed to shut the door, then they stayed outside – they would have liked to see what papa dear did to Chick-Chick, doubtless he would cut off first her one hand, then the other, so she couldn't steal anymore, but staying inside the house seemed ill advised, as they knew how swift his hand was, how quick he was to dole out slaps, hits, kicks, everything. Little Chick-Chick still did not know what to expect. She didn't even cry, she just stood there stiffly, her mouth open; if she'd dared, she would have laughed that papa dear didn't want to take her into his arms now and pet her with his great, red-haired paws, like a little cat, which it wasn't all right to tell anyone about. Then she saw how Dudás, because even though they called him papa dear, other people who didn't live with them called him Dudás – and now she really couldn't call him papa dear, but only Dudás ... how Dudás took a glowing ember from the cookstove, and said:

"Hold out your hands."

Mrs. Dudás was frightened too, more so than her husband, and she yammered:

"What are you gonna do to her?"

"I'm gonna teach this pig not to steal anymore. Hold her hands. Hold her fingers together and keep her hands still."

Mrs. Dudás instinctively obeyed him, she grabbed the girl's small hands so that her fingers nestled together in the hollow of her hand.

"Hold them so that I can set the ember down on them. She won't be stealing again, by God ..."

And Mrs. Dudás held the girl's small hands between her thumb and index finger, like little flowers, and Dudás put the ember on them, but Mrs. Dudás felt the burning of the ember on her skin first, she dropped the girl's hands and flung the ember from her own hand.

"Ouch!"

Little Chick-Chick only now sensed the burning on her fingertips, at the nails of her tiny hands, and began to scream.

"You gonna steal again? You gonna steal? Gonna let the cow trample the grape vines again? Huh?"

"I'm sorry, papa dear, I won't st-st-steal again."

She shook over her entire little body, and threw herself at the man's ugly, hairy hands, and wanted to hold them and kiss them.

Then father Dudás took the cellar key down from the hook and left them. He went outside, even leaving the door open.

"My sweet little girl," mama dear yammered apologetically, "it's not all right to steal, didn't you know that? I told papa dear because I'm too weak to teach you. But he's taught you a hard lesson, come here, come, I'll put a little cloth with sour cream on your hands. You see, my hand burned even more, 'cause I was looking out for you, when I saw that papa dear was gonna put the ember on you, I pushed your weak little fingers away a bit, and look, the ember barely touched your finger tips, but you can look at my hand, my flesh even smoked, it burned so much when he pressed the ember down, so don't steal anymore, my child, 'cause that's the greatest sin.

Don't take what isn't yours. Here everything belongs to others as far as you're concerned; 'cause here Rózsika, Julika, Mariska, they can take whatever they want, you know, they're all at home here, my child, but you can't take anything from anywhere in the world, 'cause nothing whatsoever belongs to you. Your skin, that's yours, but nothing else is yours."

"The shirt's mine," Chick-Chick said tearfully.

This caused Mrs. Dudás to erupt in terrible anger, and she forgot the nice, kind words she'd been saying:

"What's yours? What's yours?" And she grasped the girl from both sides of her head and shook her. "What's yours, you brat? ..."

"The shirt's mine!" the little girl screamed.

"Oooh, what a snake. Is it worth it for a body to subject herself to death by fire for this deviousness? When this filthy wretch can think of nothing but what belongs to her?"

"The melons are yours, and the shirt's mine," the little girl said, stamping her foot, "but you gave my shirt to Rózsi that the manor lady brought for me."

Second Psalm

All week long they could get no use out of the little girl.

Here tiny fingers hurt constantly, especially the middle finger on her right hand and the thumb on her left hand. The large burns there could not suffer touching, they never stopped hurting, they tingled and stung, and the softest breath moving across them sent shooting pains deep within.

None was sadder for it than Borisa. No one took her out to the field where she so loved to graze.

In the mornings the boys cut corn for her before they went to work, then mama dear scolded the little girl incessantly while she used her own aching hands to feed the young, green cornstalks to the cow. She berated Chick-Chick not just because she had to do the work, but also because the cornstalks now had to serve as animal feed.

"You should've croaked in your mother's belly," she griped as she came and went.

"I can't stand to look at this lazy bitch.

chicken from Pest.

outa my sight ..."

In this way she grumbled whenever she glimpsed the little girl at the end of the house, as she was always perched there in the sun, already sensing the approach of colder days – weakened by all her crying, she had no desire to run about, and in her nakedness she sensed the fog more keenly, the fog having already arrived, especially early in the day.

"Go to the field already, I've had it with you – tomorrow you're goin'.

so I don't have to look at you day in day out

you're not much to look at

the devil's horse should carry you off."

But Chick-Chick longed to. To go out to the field. So mama dear's bluster didn't bother her, it just made her laugh, only her fingers hurt, but when the throbbing subsided, nothing bothered her. Mama dear's hand hurt too, poor thing. Big black scabs formed along her fingers, she couldn't stand dunking them in water, that was worst of all, but she couldn't avoid it. Someone had to mix the slop; when she drew up the water, some always sloshed onto her hand, and she threw up her arms and swore. It hurt her so badly, the poor dear, that she constantly had to take it out on someone or something, but in her anger she often didn't know what she was doing. But someone had to do the cooking:

"Who'll do it if I don't
God damn me to hell
reduced to this by that little wretch
why I deserved this hell ..."

Not a moment passed without her finding reason to grumble. Chick-Chick just played in the dust with her bandaged hands, it wouldn't hurt the cloth, they were as black as the dirt she was picking at, after all. And once the sour cream inside had dried, then the bandaging prickled her, it had gotten hard, clumpy, rough and nubbly. So she tore it from her hands, ripping at it with her teeth because she couldn't use her fingers, but by now she was so eager for her eyes to meet up with her tiny hands that she gnawed and chewed like a little mouse, careful to keep from hurting herself, until her fingers suddenly peered out from the cloth.

She just stared.

Her fingers were terribly swollen. Big, sinister, black wounds marred each fingertip, she couldn't tell which was worst off.

In that moment mama dear noticed her.

Oh my, she got terribly angry.

Poor mama dear was only ever angry.

"Why did you chew that off, you shameless wretch, I didn't put that on you so you could just rip it off. A body breaks herself in two from all the work, and all I get with this one is just more work? Don't I have enough to trouble myself with, what was I thinking, saddling myself with you, you ...

You, you.

you curse you

oh you

come here, let's fix it then

as though I didn't suffer enough already

God had to saddle me with this yet too

oh you

in the morning I'm sending you off to the field

you and Borisa

if you rip off the bandage

that's what I stuff you with food for

that's how you thank me

you curse

oh you curse

o you"

And little Chick-Chick recalled that tomorrow she was to go to the field together with Borisa. That was for the better, as mama dear would just keep up her litany of complaints, there would be no end to them, which wasn't so bad considering that all her griping was meant to quell her own pain, the poor thing couldn't run around yelling oh, how my hand hurts, oh, my sore hand, that's why she went around yelling oh, you curse, it's your doing, you, oh, you, you …

Bori simply lost her head. Presumably she noticed that little Chick-chick couldn't grasp the switch. She can only hold it under her arm and drive the cow like that. She gestures with it, helplessly flapping the long switch about, but she can't grasp it in her little hands, it hurts too much.

The tears just roll down her face, and she sings.

She sings without cease, she sings everything that comes to mind, and goes along behind the cow, who goes where she likes. After having been away from the field for several days, who knew how many, she wants to taste everything, and runs like a fool.

Chick-Chick tells her off like mama dear does her: "Borisa, Borisa, boohoriissaa
   I'll beat you
   I'll strike you dead
   the hell with you
   Booorrii"

Fortunately her little feet don't hurt, her small bare feet take no notice of the stubble, the thorns, nothing, they like wading through the dirt, especially where it's fine like dust.

She holds her bread under the one arm, the switch under the other. That's how she runs after the cow.

Always to the grape vines, the grape vines.

She wants to trample another vine.

Fortunately no one is around.

Papa dear went off to work somewhere else. Doubtless he went to the cornfield with the boys, because he's nowhere to be seen.

"Borisa, stay away from the grape vines. Bori."

That afternoon the children came out. Mama dear had sent them out to help tend the cow.

"Come to the grape vines, let's go to the grape vines and eat some grapes."

"Not me, they're sour."

"Kadarcs's are sweet. Ripe and sweet – let's go to Kadarcs's grape vines."

"There's no gate."

"We'll dig our way in."

They started digging. Their little black hands scratched and scraped like so many moles, until the smallest of them could slip through. Chick-Chick was made to crawl through, and once she was in, she noticed that she'd scratched her hands bloody on the hedge. She sat on the mound beneath the vine, it wouldn't occur to her to eat anything, to take what wasn't hers. She only crawled through there because she had to and did as her siblings ordered.

But they were losing patience on the other side, with her eating in there and them getting nothing, they groused until, one after the other, they all managed to squeeze their way through. Oh, how splendid it was in there, a garden of Eden, every tree full of plums, the wormy ones had all fallen to the ground and were deliciously sweet.

Then the farmer, Kadarcs, came.

Quick, out of the grape vines!

They all managed to escape, even little Chick-Chick.

But uncle István Kadarcs climbed over the hedge and ran after them.

They ran like wild things from the grape vines; like wild little rabbits, they ducked here and there. They didn't search for the gate, they hid.

The farmer Kadarcs ran menacingly after them.

"Who's the littlest among you?"

All of them ran off, leaving little Chick-Chick to stare up at the big black man, whimpering in fright.

"You stay here, the others go home."

"Why do I stay here? I'll get b-beat-t-ten."

"Go home, all of you, everyone, go home!"

Chick-Chick screamed:

"Look after Borisa, she'll trample the wheat!"

She had to take charge, she understood her craft. She was responsible. She didn't know what responsibility was, she just did it.

Farmer Kadarcs merely stared at the girl, guarding her like a little lamb. He stood with his legs apart, his hands in the pockets of his velvet trousers, and laughed like a wolf.

Then he bent down to pick a bunch of grapes.

"Those aren't yours!"

The big man burst out laughing. This little squirt was teaching him about mine and thine? Just to get her goat, he reached in among the grapes.

"Don't hurt them!" the little girl screamed – "I'll burn your fingers!"

"What'll you do?"

"Burn them!"

The man's mouth hung open. My, how the little dog snarls.

"Grrr-rufff!" he teased her as he would a dog, and he reached for the grapes as though afraid the child would strike him, flinching to keep his head out of harm's way.

He even put a few tart grapes in his mouth, asking:

"The plums were yours?"

"The plums are fine, 'cause they're not ours, but the grapes aren't, 'cause they're ours. Those are papa dear's! Mama dear's! The children's! Don't hurt the grapes!"

Farmer Kadarcs was having a grand time. Again he plucked, again he ate.

Chick-Chick lost her head like a rabid little dog, forgot her pain, lunged at the large man, grabbed his hand and bit into it.

She didn't care that her fingers on both hands ached, she just hung on to the big man's paw, trying to bite into it, but her fragile little teeth were no match for the hard, calloused hand.

Farmer Kadarcs grabbed the little naked girl, roaring with laughter, he lifted her up from the ground by her leg like a frog, and let her dangle in front of him.

"So you're protecting Dudás's grapes for him?

Then I'll hire you.

up – "

He flung her up into the air, the child flew, not knowing when she would plop onto the ground, but just as she was about to, farmer Kadarcs caught her, hurled her up high again, and played with her as though she were a ball.

Then he held her to his mouth and blew into her belly, playing her like a trumpet, brrr, the child trembled in fear.

"Don't hurt me!"

Farmer Kadarcs went off with the child; took her with him; took her into his vineyard:

"So now I've got you! now I've got you! now you can't run away from me.

do you like bread with honey?

do you like sweets ...

you dirty little brat ...

now I'm gonna break all your bones, gonna eat you up, swallow you, devour you ...

I've been salivating after you for a long time now

do ya know who I am? I'm uncle Rudi, I'm a soldier, I just got back from the front, did ya know that?"

But of course Chick-Chick knew he was uncle Pista Kadarcs, the neighbor to the left.

"Uncle Pista!" she yelled at him.

"Uncle Rudi!" the man laughed.

"Uncle Pista!"

"Won't you shut your trap! Didn't you hear that I'm uncle Rudi? You!"

Laughing wildly, he smashed and twisted the child as though she were a willow rod who felt nothing, as bendable as a rope.

"Don't you like uncle Rudi? Oh you no one's child!"

The children had already run quite far, but they kept looking back: they would have liked to know what was happening with Chick-Chick.

All of a sudden they heard a blood-curdling scream. In his wild shenanigans the crude man heaved the child over a stake – immediately she was dripping with blood.

But he didn't care. He just threw her on the ground.

"Go home. They're waiting for you."

Chick-Chick reached behind her where it hurt and the blood was flowing, and ran bare foot across the field. There was no one around, only a little bird hopping along the huge stubblefield.

Maybe the other birds just looked up, but otherwise not a single soul bothered with her.

No one was waiting for her. No one to make things better, to heal her – horrible.

She just ran, bleeding, the blood dripping over her heels. He hadn't even bandaged her, uncle Pista … uncle Rudi? …

Dusk was already settling when they drove the cow home, all of the children ambling along with her, even Chick-Chick.

"Why are you all bloody?"

"The stake poked me."

"What stake?"

"Uncle Rudi."

"What uncle Rudi?"

But she didn't know what to say, she felt only one thing, namely how good it was that she'd caught up with her siblings. How nice it was to seek refuge among them, to be with them. How nice that she was no longer far from them, she was with them, she didn't care that her blood was dripping, she just cried quietly and happily that her siblings weren't mistreating her now, they felt sorry for her. She never knew that before, maybe she sensed now for the first time that, when you're being tormented in a strange place, there's nothing better than escaping into the midst of your siblings. She thought that man would kill her, slinging her around like that, like a ball, but she was no ball, she was a little girl.

She couldn't say anything, she just cried and cried, but not sad tears, rather glad tears, as she had once again cheated death.

The poor thing, she doesn't even know what death is, and yet she senses that, when a person is cast away among strangers, that's death; and returning back home among those with whom you belong, because they are yours, your siblings, that's life. Something warmed her inside, and she sensed that things were good between her and her siblings, even in the absence of physical contact. At home, mama dear, too, just looked at the little girl, she washed her, bandaged her, without saying so much as a single unkind word, not even: the devil take you, all you bring me is bother. On this day little Chick-Chick didn't even get beaten.

She slept together with Rozi next to the oven. Now mama dear said:

"Leave Chick-Chick alone now. Don't kick her. Her behind hurts."

This so warmed Chick-Chick's little heart that it nearly burst. Mama dear loves her after all. She won't allow the others to kick her.

And she was truly proud, and she pampered her wound, which admittedly smarted. Mama dear had bandaged it with salt water, and the salt and the pain coursed through it, but she buried her small, grimy face in her little black hands, and cried inwardly, and rejoiced that she was so very fortunate to have the sort of injury that made even mama dear feel for her.

She was proud that now something truly awful had happened to her, because when papa dear had burned her with the ember before, mama dear hadn't felt so badly for her.

She was half asleep when she heard:

"It was him, it was Pista! Rudi, the heck with Rudi! Pista Kadarcs was the beast, he should go to hell."

Chick-Chick drank in these words. Now for the first time she wasn't the one who should go to hell. For the very first time, mama dear was cursing another, and for her sake, she's cursing István Kadarcs.

"He's gonna pay for that," papa dear growled. "I'll show him."

"Filthy pig, he should've croaked in his mother's womb," mama dear swore.

For once in her life she, too, can be happy. If only she knew what happiness is, as she doesn't even know the word. She merely senses how nice it is when strangers do really bad things to a person, because then everyone at home looks at you differently and feels sorry for you.

She would have liked to get down and crouch at mama dear's feet so she could kiss them. She would dearly have loved to slip all the way beneath mother's blanket and wrap her two little arms around the woman's poor, withered neck, but she dared not move, as she feared that this great niceness would evaporate.

So she simply hugged herself, she caressed her little face with her two little hands such that her face stroked the tiny hands upon which it lay. And it was so nice that mama dear covered her with a warm shawl, but it wasn't only the warm shawl that did her good, but how nicely and carefully mother wrapped it all around her, so that the wind could not blow in on her anywhere ...

She may never have fallen asleep so nicely in her entire life.

She was happy, and she dreamed that mama dear offered her a cup of milk:

and *she drank it up and enjoyed the milk!*

and it was very nice. So she wondered how it could be that someone wouldn't like milk? When her mother's milk tasted so very, very good to her ...

So very good, that it woke her up.

But she soon fell back asleep, dreaming of nothing but good and lovely things.

Third Psalm

The dawns grew ever chillier, but a person gets used to that, right, Chick-Chick? The naked girl shivered as she went out with the cow, day after day.

Only it was strange, before no one ever saw her, but now no matter when she followed after the cow, she only ever met the eyes of men. If a farm wagon came past her and the driver snapped toward her head with his whip from his seat, if someone came towards her with horse and wagon, from afar she had to escape up the muddy ditch, lurking between the slender acacias wondering, was someone going to hurt her? The autumn mornings, the autumn evenings were studded full of men's eyes. All of them laughed at her, all of them mocked her, what did they want with her? She shot hostile, spiteful, sullen looks back at them, puffed up her little cheeks and hissed at them like a wildcat.

Their gazes even penetrated the ground, stinging and singeing her, even when she turned her back she knew that the one with the great moustache now had his eyes trained on her. But only right when she saw it, as otherwise it never entered her mind, she played and sang, she never stopped singing, loudly, at the top of her voice, she just sang, singing whatever met her ear – she quickly picked it up and gave it voice.

The children were often outside, mama dear chased them out when they returned home from school, or didn't go there at all, so they could be with the cow and not bother her at home. If her siblings were there, Chick-Chick stood, drew up her little mouth into a frown, watched them, and was jealous when they told her: look after the cow.

She always had to watch the cow and follow her around, she could not forget for a single moment that she had only to watch, to look after Borisa.

In play the children hitched Chick-Chick to the handcart, they all got in and she had to pull them:

"Giddyup, Chick-Chick ... Giddyup ...," and they snapped their little whip.

And Chick-Chick started to cry:

"You're heav-vy, I'm not a horse."

Sometimes she wanted to sit in the cart too, but they wouldn't allow it, not that, never, she couldn't sit in the handcart, who ever heard of such a thing, that the horse should sit in the wagon, or the state child in the toy cart.

But it was dreadfully hard, with six of them sitting in there.

And then there was the whip, the coachman sat up front, and if she went slowly, she got smacked, but that was no reason to cry. Of course if mama dear struck her, then she couldn't cry enough, since that was a punishment.

One day they played draw-well.

When mama dear wasn't at home, that's when they played that game.

They got into the bucket and lowered each other all the way down to the water.

But they didn't lower Rózsi, and that evening Rózsi told on them. Oh, did they get it for that.

That's how it all ended, with a beating.

And it was such a good game, too, how they rolled when they got tipped out of the bucket.

That's why she loved her little girl, Rózsi, because she squealed about everything; when it came to Chick-Chick, mama dear said: "that imp? she'd never divulge a single thing!"

And she didn't divulge it either when they milked the cow, out in the field with the children, in the young wheat. And she was the one who'd played the most important role. All day long she'd grazed the cow on the young wheat, but she'd kept having to chase her around to keep her from gobbling up all the young plants and trampling them, and the children came out to her, and one of them said they should milk the cow.

"Wait, I'll show you how mama dear does it."

They first went to the ditch in search of an old pot, there were always busted pots lying there in which meals had been brought to the harvesters and which had ended up broken.

This they washed in the lake; then all four of them crouched down beneath Borisa and yanked on her teats.

"Not like that, not like that, I'll show you how mama dear does it."

In the end Borisa tired of the honor being bestowed upon her, and when the pot was already half full, she kicked, she jigged, causing the four children to scatter and knocking the pot from their hands.

"You, Chick-Chick, what's wrong with this cow?" mama dear asked that evening during milking.

"Something wrong?"

"Did somebody milk her? She's giving so little."

"Like I would have milked her, seeing as how I don't even like milk, I gag at the smell of it."

"Then you didn't graze her right. You tethered her, you brat, and the poor cow went hungry."

"Where would I have tied her to?"

"You went thieving in the grape vines, no doubt. Your father did well to burn your fingers, you've got some very sticky fingers there."

Miska, the biggest boy, stood there then, his legs spread apart, and laughed out loud. She didn't dare say anything to him, as he was already big, a round-headed youth, and sometimes he just stood staring at Chick-Chick, his mouth open wide, and neighed loudly like a horse, then he said:

"Damn!"

And he shook his head and neighed again, then he went off, forgot her, and finished his work. But as soon as he saw her, again he opened his mouth, ready to neigh, again he shook his head, and he neighed. What was it that caught his eye on her, as each time he neighed it was as though he was seeing her for the first time and noticing something on her, even though she'd grown up here, in front of his eyes.

She went out of her way to get into everyone's good graces, as her sole wish was to be regarded the same as the others. Of course that wasn't possible, as the others were different, they had clothes and shoes too, while she went about like the pig or the dog, wearing her own skin. But she grasped at every opportunity to demonstrate that there was no difference among them. She did just the same as her siblings, for example if they didn't get enough milk bread, even though there was plenty, she got up during the night and silently opened the drawer, took out the milk bread, and gave some to the others as well. Rózsi didn't say anything, because she got to eat some too, so she didn't tattle about this, but she did about the other things.

When they'd played the well game, too, they'd exclaimed to her: "Judas, think you're gonna get an Easter egg?"

"Yeah, Judas, think you're gonna get an Easter egg? You won't be gettin' any Easter egg – just a swift kick!"

But it wasn't Rózsi they'd kicked, it was Chick-Chick, as though she'd been the tattler. Whenever mama dear didn't see them, they kicked her. Even Miska and Jóska ran after her and kicked her with their bare feet.

"Waaah!"

But the boys weren't so bad, they weren't kicking her to hurt her, they were just kicking her. And laughing.

"He's teasing me, he's teasing me," she said, running after mama dear like a calf after its mother, hanging on her wherever she went.

"Be still. And what're you all teasing her for?"

The games were unforgettable, the beatings too. And the suffering above all.

But a person also hangs on to the joys.

"It was always the boys who defended me the best. Come 'ere, Chick-Chick."

She'll never forget that beautiful country. Not a single building around, just a little farmstead. Wherever a person looked, nothing was seen but wheat.

Just a naked pup in the wheatfield.

And here a boy snarls at her, there too. Always laughing. And biting.

When mama dear went into town to shop, then no one needed to go out with the cow. The cow stayed indoors in the stable, she had to be fed. There was some nice feed corn.

As for Chick-Chick, at such times she set about cleaning the entire house. My, how her little hands flew, she swept, she scrubbed out every nook and cranny, and redid the earthen floor. She drew her little hands evenly across the yellow mud so as not to leave any streaks, oh, God forbid that a single stroke of her hand should be visible.

Then she dusted everything that was on the chest of drawers, but she didn't remove anything, as the first time she got into trouble because she got a piece of porcelain down somehow and couldn't figure out how to put it back. Until mama dear came home: "What did you do? Stand on the stool – what a stupid girl. Can't even get up on the stool." From that point on every piece came down and went back up, left its spot and returned to it, but it also happened that, when mama dear returned home, she looked around, then grew quite serious: "I've got me a girl who really knows how to clean." And she kissed the little state child.

But when she dried off a plate and didn't know just where to put it away:

"You piece of shit, put that plate back right, what're you looking at, what're you trying to be? A fine little lady?"

But Chick-Chick didn't want to be a fine little lady, and she cried bitterly that they were shaming her with such a thing, she wanted to be a seamstress, she sewed constantly and made off with every needle she could lay her hands on. But it's worth knowing that in the typical village home there is only one needle in the entire house. If that one can't be found, there is no other, especially not out there on a farmstead, where such a thing can't even be bought. But Chick-Chick had made off with it and was always sewing doll clothes according to the latest fashion. And she always got into trouble over the needle, if it disappeared, they scolded her alone:

"I haven't seen it."

She didn't let on where it was, because if she were to give it back, then she would surely never see it again her entire life. Buck naked, she sewed fashionable clothes.

❦

The reason you don't have any clothes is 'cause they give you paper clothes, and Rózsi wears them out so fast.

To hell with them, why do they send such rags?

She feared she would soon have to wear the rags. The ones she slept on in the corner.

Raggedy old rags, the worn out cast-offs of the other children. Sleeping on them was disgusting enough, covering herself with them even worse.

She'd never left the farmstead, just like the little piglet. Until she was seven she never even saw the church tower.

One time relatives came in a wagon, and she was struck with wonder: they had relatives in this world? She herself had no mother, no father, no parent whatsoever, and no relatives either, while these kids had a father, a mother, and even relatives, too. She found that terribly unfair.

In fact she didn't believe it, she thought they were just conning her. Taking away from her what was hers – could be the relative was a good person, so she snuggled up to him ...

"Whose little calf are you, then?" the relative asked.

"Nobody's, uncle relative."

"No mother?"

"No, just mama dear."

"Who brought you into the world, then?"

"I'm just the state's."

The nice relative laughed and looked at the child clad in rags. But he took no particular interest in her, only noting that this sort of thing exists too.

"Those Dudáses have got it good, they pick a state child up out of the dirt, feed her for three months, pocket enough money to buy a young pig, then after that the child allowance covers all the feed needed to fatten it … How old are you, little one?"

"I don't know."

"You don't even know that? You look plenty old to be in school … However many pigs are on the farm here, they've all been fattened off of this."

"Better that than getting brined, like at the Tatárs," the other relative said. "How? Everyone left the house, only the nine-year-old stayed behind with the state child. So the nine-year-old told the little state child once they were alone: 'Come, I'll brine you.'

"With that he grabbed the child, and slaughtered her like his papa did the pig. He stabbed her, cut off her hands and feet, gutted her, and brined it all just as it was.

"The parents came home that evening, then they asked, where's the state child?

"The nine-year-old said: 'In the trough, I brined her.'

"But for a nine-year-old to have so little sense that he hears the other cry and it doesn't hurt him that it hurts her."

Chick-Chick listened aghast: could they brine her too?

But she calmed down, because she wouldn't let that happen. She'd sooner brine another, Rózsi for sure, who was wearing her clothes. But she wouldn't hurt her when she did it.

She even went over to her and caressed the girl, who was no older than she was, but already went to school. It was true, if there was only one shirt because the woman in charge of her only gave them one shirt, and that was made of paper, then the two of them couldn't run around together in the one shirt, that was for sure.

"You have a prettier shirt, my child," the women said out in the field, "you have the prettiest shirt of all, right?"

But it was nice at night. During the winter in the snug little corner by the oven when it was heated up nice and warm, but if the oven was cold, then beside the chest of drawers, the four of them together on the broad wooden bed. They romped and played until they fell asleep, the ailing woman just blustered, grumbled, hit them.

"What are you doing, you, when will you finally be quiet?"

Once an apple fell from the chest and ended up on the bed, that got that ants' nest moving, they started swarming like maggots, like chicks when one of them finds something good, it doesn't eat it, it runs off with it until the second one grabs it, then this one runs off, loses it, now the third one runs off with it, in this way the children ran frantically after each other over the apple:

"Are you crazy, have you gone crazy in there – may the devil shred you up into kindling, you curs."

In no time someone has snatched the apple, only for the next one to grab it and bite off a chunk, suddenly everyone was gnawing at it, their crunching could be heard in the dark, meanwhile they were choking with laughter. Oh dear, they weren't allowed to eat the apples, the apples were placed there atop the chest for decoration, but no one would have reached for one for anything in the world, only this time the apple fell down to them, that was different.

Mama dear got up to see what the devil they were up to, nothing suspicious met her eyes, she couldn't look into their bellies, she just beat them one and all; so they would truly go to sleep, she summoned all her strength and slapped their plump behinds so hard it would smart twenty years down the road when they remembered it.

After that the children quieted down, slowly they fell asleep, if one of them made a peep, immediately she threatened: "What are you doing?"

"Where's my comb, haven't you seen it?"

"Of course, mama dear, it's running off to the stable, with Borisa."

When in fact Maris was combing herself with it.

"What the devil were you stinking kids up to last night. What were you nibbling on."

She goes up to the chest of drawers, and yells:

"One of the apples is missing! You ate it. Didn't you? Who took it? I'll cut off their fingers. Was it you, you thief?"

Chick-Chick excused herself, laughing:

"It came down on its own, mama dear, truly, no one did anything to it, it just came down."

"It what? What came down?"

"The apple."

"In a word, you did it. Just wait, you, now I'll finish you."

The hens laid their eggs, they were forever digging for eggs beneath the heaps of straw, the stacks of hay – nevertheless once in spring a hen shows up with little chicks in tow.

"Oh to hell with you, that's how you collect eggs? You scamps, we could easily have sold those, now what am I gonna do with these rascals, I'll just be stuck feeding them."

But the little hatchlings grew up, they were delightful, cute little peepers, oh how lovely, but when they were grown, right, mama dear thought how good it would be to sell them at the market. It would never have occurred to her to butcher them, God forbid, that was akin to taking a human life, the chickens had to be sold at the market, there was no use raising a fuss about it, the feed cost her next to nothing, after all.

And Borisa, she said one evening, was going to calve.

My, what a commotion there was! No one went to bed, everyone stayed awake, the children all hovered around the barn door, every one of them refusing to go to bed.

"Go and run over to Mágócs's, send someone to help, since Borisa's calving. We can't rely on your father, the devil knows what he's up to."

She would never have said anything bad about her husband, because deep down she was afraid he would leave her. And things were such that, since she'd become ill, he'd gotten that much worse, he'd just as soon have her die; as long as she was young, and pretty, he'd just sired child after child, but now that he couldn't so much as touch her, he wouldn't hesitate to tear her away from her children. But for that reason she keeps her mouth shut around him, no matter how he acts or what he does to her, if he beats her, if he cleaves her in two, so afraid is she that the man will one day get fed up with all this fighting and squabbling, that he'll hightail it to another woman's side, there are plenty of them on the puszta, widows, desirable women, and being left without a man, without a husband, oh God, without this swine of a man, then what's the point of all the children, there's no point, no point in living, then she might as well die, might as well go to the dogs, go to rot in hell. But as it is, no matter how far she's fallen, how weak she's become, she still has enough strength, because she has enough desire. And somehow she'll get Borisa through the birth, even if the man is boozing it up in the house, lying there drunk like a corpse, Borisa still has to get the job done.

István Kadarcs came.

"What's going on? Greetings."

"Oh, oh! István, come and help, it's almost out — poor Borisa's just about all done in."

Snickering in excitement, the children watched the events unfold, even Chick-Chick huddled among the others. István Kadarcs looked over at her, his eyes flashing at the sight of the naked girl.

"Who was with her when she was with the bull? This one here?"

Mama dear looked at him angrily, István Kadarcs was this Rudi person during the summer who'd inflicted the bloody wound on the girl, but she needed his help, and since decent people don't speak about such things, she overlooked it, instead scolding the child: "The devil take you, go on inside, don't stand around here underfoot, you."

The children had only one thought: the calf is coming, we're getting a calf. And when it came: damn, it's ugly.

But this time the new critter wasn't so spritely as last year, when Bori had played the prank of giving birth to a little bull. That was great fun. He couldn't be subdued, they'd had to tie a rope around his neck to keep him from running off into the wild. You should have seem him jump about, he jumped so high, it made everyone laugh.

But now they just looked on wide-eyed as István Kadarcs took off his damp shirt and used it to wipe the little animal down, until its body puffed up as nicely as a sweet-smelling lump of bread dough in a basket.

Chick-Chick looked on with a grimace, petrified and fearing the worst, when the little calf got up on its legs, and mama dear sprinkled a little water between her eyes, then pronounced:

"Well thank God, we're gonna call her Moo-Cow."

Chick-Chick looked on and shuddered, repulsed by this man who was splattered all over with blood.

The next morning, the little calf was as pretty as could be, and before the children went off to school, they looked on in the stable as Borisa licked her baby clean. They grabbed her leg and laughed to see her hobble, while Borisa tried to break the rope.

"What in God's name are you doing to her, just you wait, if she croaks, then you're in for it, father will chop off your heads, 'cause I'll tell him what you did."

Chick-Chick wasn't afraid of the calf by day, but in this moment she believed her mama dear really would carry out her threat to tell papa dear, just like she had when she'd stolen the melon. She could almost feel how her head was lowered onto a stump, and chopped off at the neck.

Jóska, the oldest boy, said:

"Mama's gonna have a calf too, another one."

The children burst out laughing.

Chick-Chick didn't understand:

"Can't you see it? Just look at her, right?"

Chick-Chick looked at her, but still couldn't see it, right?

"Can I give little Borisa a little potato soup, mama dear?"

But their mother didn't answer, as she was busy pacifying big Borisa with calming words of comfort: "No, no, my sweet little beauty, pretty Bori, my precious girl, calm down, I'll show those evil brats what for, if they so much as touch your sweet baby one more time, you poor thing, poor sweet animal, making such a fuss over so little, and causing a person all this bother ... Nooo, no my little Bori, nooo ..."

Jóska had already fetched a bowl of potato soup, they'd had it for breakfast and he didn't like it. The children looked on and giggled, wondering, what would the little calf think of that, would she like it?

Their mother struck at them, dispersing them, and Chick-Chick stared at yesterday's blood, still lingering there among the straw, she saw it and her head spun.

She couldn't eat the spinach either, it was too much like something the calf would have produced. Later it just flowed out of the calf, the lovely, pure, watery spinach. If mama dear cooked spinach, they said: "We don't like calf spinach. Tender, fresh, calf spinach:

splat splat splat
calfy runs, you eat that"

But no evening passed without an argument. There were times when mama dear escaped without bleeding, but it always started with: "Now I'll end you."

On this evening, however, papa dear came home very tired and angry, having worked all day long in the fields, breaking corn and hauling it in with the big wagon. Jóska had also been working alongside his father, and they hadn't sent Miska to school that day either. On such days, when there was so much work, father Dudás was terribly ill-tempered, as they would never hire extra hands, instead working their own selves to death.

"Now I'll end you."

In that moment the children came into the house to cut themselves a piece of bread, but mama dear dared not come inside. Papa dear looked at them, then set to roaring:

"What do you want here, you bastards?"

He pointed at them with the big knife: "I'll slice you all up!" and they ran screaming from the room, but it always went like that, even in winter, with mama dear freezing at the foot of the haystack, since which time she was always coughing and sickly. Now, too, all of them ran off wherever they could, fearing he would murder them in cold blood. They ran across to the haystack, there they cooled their heels, thinking they would have to spend the night there.

"Mama dear, come up here, mama dear, come up here," Chick-Chick whispered as they heard father bellowing inside, and doubtless scared out of her mind, the mother climbed up the ladder to the top of the haystack, then the children even pushed the ladder away from the rick.

How shaken they were. Dudás was in no rush, he just kept thundering as always, meanwhile fetching wine from the cellar, which he drank. Then he came back out so he could yell but good. "Where's your mother?" he howled, fortifying his bluster with ugly words.

Renewed fright coursed then through the children. A ghost came in a white sheet, uttering ghostly moans, hoots, and howls over them, frightening them: "Chick-Chick ... Chi-i-i-ck-Chi-i-i-ck."

It was already late, and dark too, as there was no moonlight.

"Papa dear, papa dear, the ghost is here," the poor children shrieked. Mrs. Dudás didn't dare descend from the haystack, as she was more afraid of her husband than of the ghost, so from her perch up on top she merely told the children to go in the house and tell their father.

It was little Chick-Chick whom they shoved inside, as they'd noticed that papa tolerated Chick-Chick best when he was drunk – it didn't occur to them why Chick-Chick might be more afraid of him than of the ghost. So the little girl went inside, and she yelled distinctly into papa dear's ear, that the ghost was in the yard, in a white sheet, screaming: "Chick-Chick."

Dudás opened the drawer and removed the revolver from it, went outside, then he shot into the white-shrouded ghost, the ghost fell down, and lay there in the yard. As the spirit fell, father cursed in relief, turned around and went back into the house, then lay down to go to sleep. In the meantime, the children had all fled into the house, now he chased them out: "Get out, you miserable little shits, I don't need you, go, there's no ghost anymore, out with you, but your mother should get in here, 'cause if she doesn't come, I'll crack her skull with the threshing flail." But the children ran outside and told their mother not to go in the house, instead they climbed up to her, covered her with straw to keep her from freezing in the night, while they themselves cowered in the kitchen, marking time until morning; they fell asleep huddled together in front of the oven, and little Chick-Chick started up every minute, fearing the ghost would come, but that was already stone-dead, and lay there in the yard until morning came and papa dear finally got up, went out and found it:

"What's this character doing here?" he asked.

The children told him it was the spirit that he'd shot during the night for frightening them so. Dudás lifted the sheet:

"Oh my fucking God, where's your mother? Rozi! Do you hear me, God damn it!?"

But they didn't tell him where she was. And mama dear was loathe to move a muscle.

"If my wife doesn't show up," Dudás shouted, "I'll shoot myself dead on the spot," and he aimed the revolver at his head.

The children were horrified and started screaming: "Mama dear, dear mother, please come down, papa dear's gonna kill himself!"

Only little Chick-Chick didn't shout, she just looked on, trembling, her teeth chattering, her belly had even turned blue, from which Dudás could tell that she was most fearful for mama dear, especially as the children told him: "Chick-Chick said to, Chick-Chick thought of climbing up on top of the haystack."

But when the mother climbed down from the rick, nothing bad happened, Dudás just said to his wife:

"I'm going in to the parish hall, in the meantime keep an eye on this sorry carcass."

When he left, the children had to stay by the corpse, Chick-Chick especially, as the others were freezing, only she was never allowed to freeze, nor to be hungry, nor be afraid, whatever was bad she always had to bear, and now she had to stay there all morning long, because otherwise the dogs would assail the poor dead ghost; so there was no one to drive out the cattle, as the children went off to school, Rózsi stayed home, but the cow couldn't be entrusted to her, therefore mama dear grew very angry that those poor animals must spend the entire day inside the stable because of such a sorry man, why in hell would István Kadarcs show up over here in a ghost suit, now he'd gotten his. But now mama dear was terribly afraid that they'd punish papa dear, but papa dear was very lucky, because he told the judge that: "My children feared for their lives, so I defended them."

Papa dear returned home from the parish hall, and said at the top of his voice: "If it weren't for these children, they would have locked me up, lightning should strike that lousy carcass, but now, mother, he has to be buried." A smirk flashed across his face. Now he was so sweet, as he was whenever he allowed his sober self to indulge in a growl. At such times he was truly loveable. They took the dead man out to the village in the wagon, to the morgue, from there he was buried, and nothing bad came of it all, but they never told the children who the spirit was, only: "It was a ghost, so ..." Only Chick-Chick knew that it was uncle Kadarcs. He wouldn't heave her onto a stake again. And papa dear shot him out of anger, because he recognized him. People came over from their farmsteads, all of them laughed: served the beast right.

It was nice that they worried about the orphan, it felt good that all the powerful men trained their eyes on her: served the beast right.

Little Chick-Chick grew terribly fearful after all this, so much so that she feared being alone, she constantly saw ghosts everywhere, especially as she'd had to guard the one in death, and whenever it got dark, she felt like oh, the spirit's right there, behind me, it's gonna bite me in the back. Whenever she was late driving the cattle home, because no one came for her and she had to wait for help getting the milk cow home with her calf, who shouldn't be left to such a little girl to watch, but at home there was always a dreadful amount of work, and not a soul got around to coming for the cow, then little Chick-Chick just cowered and trembled, sometimes she even sensed how some spirit or other was nipping at her back. For no one knew anything concrete about ghosts, only that they were scary, right?

But one time she was awakened during the night by mama dear's wailing, whimpering, moaning, groaning: only now papa dear wasn't cursing, he was carrying out the bucket, which was full of blood. The children awoke, they stood about and listened, lay in wait from the corners, the bed, the door.

That was the real ghost. Maybe it had returned to cause their poor mother harm.

Little Chick-Chick thought nothing, she only wondered that mother was suffering.

Fourth Psalm

After that the children just went off to school every day. What was school? Chick-Chick would have loved to go. It had to be something good, but she didn't know what, exactly, as she'd never yet left the farmstead, nor had she ever been to another farmstead, she just thought other farms must be the same as this one. Nor had she traveled on any road but the one along which she had to drive Borisa.

She frequently sat by herself in the kitchen, in the ashes, she just sat there and stared off into space. She would have liked to go into the front room, but that wasn't allowed, no one could set foot in that room but mama dear, but how dearly she would have liked to go in there and set to working, take everything down, clean it out good, wash it down, scrub it, dry it, that would have been true happiness, absolutely.

She wasn't allowed to do that, so she just sat there, not wanting to do anything else, she crouched there, alone with her thoughts in the ashes.

Papa Dudás came out and barked at her like a ruddy dog:

"You worthless scamp, go to the stable and lie down there."

But she didn't move, she didn't leave. Never. She furrowed her brow, drew her mouth into a pout, and just kept staring into space there in the ashes.

Mama dear came in from the stable, hunched over, jaundiced and gaunt and panting, with reddened face, but she did nothing besides moan and groan.

"No one loves me anymore," she said softly, "just my children. And this one, this little orphan, she loves me."

And after that she added, brooding:

"If only they wouldn't torment Borisa so."

They were just filling the straw sacks. Chick-Chick stuffed the corners of the sacks with a stirring paddle so that they were as hard as wood. Woe betide her if they weren't packed good and hard.

Every autumn, mama dear changed out the straw in the straw sacks and in the beds. The old was still good too, but dust-ridden, and the new straw had a different smell.

"Rye straw would be good, but no rye grows for us here. Only wheat, but this year the straw that produced was so nice that I just about got lost in it. Problem was, it bent over so far under its own weight that we didn't get the harvest we'd expected – well, if we get a good rain yet, then the corn will yield some oil, we'll manage one way or another. Hey, Chick-Chick, have a look, who are those people coming over there?"

The little girl opened her eyes wide, and in that same moment she ran off. Fled. She recognized the gentlewoman coming with her umbrella; she was afraid of everyone, but of none more than her, because she knew how peculiarly afraid mama dear was of this lady of the manor.

"Good day, Mrs. Dudás."

"Oh my, how do you do, ma'am, how do you do?"

"Why did Orphalina run away?"

"She's a runner, ma'am, she's a runner, poor thing."

"And why hasn't she got any clothing on?"

"It's nothing, it's just her nature, she takes them off as soon as she gets them on. No one sees her here, and it's not cold either."

"I told you already last year that I shouldn't see her naked, otherwise I'll take her away from you."

"And since then she wasn't, it's just that her smock slipped off of her. But please come inside, into the front room, ma'am."

The lady of the manor went in first. She saw that it would be very difficult to lay her hands on the child, who'd already run far across the field, her shapely little sun-tanned body twinkling in the autumn sun.

The lady of the manor proceeded with rigid, decisive steps. Mrs. Dudás followed her self-consciously, suspecting trouble.

There in the room, the lady of the manor sat down and looked around. It was clean, no doubt about that. The walls were whitewashed, the oven was painted green, neatly sectioned off, and daubed with white, green, red, and brown colors. Like a flower basket. Beams supported the ceiling, but they were painted as white as snow, and their undersides were coated brown with clean, oil-based stain. The furniture pieces were brown, old, the floor earthen, nicely polished over with clay, so that whoever didn't know better might have thought it was finished with boards. Next to the shabby, yellow-painted dining table stood light-brown hardwood chairs, and between the two windows a bench with a high back hugged the wall.

The lady of the manor didn't say a single word, she went across the entire room with an official air, seated herself between the windows in the middle of the bench, or as they called it there on the farmstead, the sofa, then sternly ordered Mrs. Dudás before her:

"Mrs. Dudás, you are faced with a serious charge. Your foster child should have been attending school for the past year, but you failed to meet the enrollment deadline."

The woman was silent.

"What is your answer to that?"

"I know nothing about that, ma'am."

"But you know that the child was born in the same year as your own daughter? I myself told you that. Do you remember how we spoke about your daughter Rózsi and the foundling being the same age? Do you? And your daughter already began to attend school last September, she's already entering the second grade. Correct?"

"Yes ma'am, she was ordered to go."

The lady of the manor would have dearly liked to settle the matter somehow, because at bottom, she was responsible for the delay, and did not now know how to bail herself out.

"Perhaps the child was ill?"

"Yes, ma'am, she's always ill, and a little backward."

"Then this year likewise she should already have been enrolled, but you are a very helpless woman, and neglected it. Be glad that I came to you before the authorities held you responsible, as the punishment for this is severe."

But Mrs. Dudás had already begun to worry that, if Chick-Chick must be sent to school, then she needs clothes and underwear, and what she received from the state was used up to the last remnant.

"How do things stand with the child's cognitive development?"

"She's a little dense, a little stupid. She'll never amount to anything."

"I'll make a note of that," said the lady of the manor. "What I don't like, as it is intolerable, is that I found the child without clothes on just now."

"She doesn't tolerate having clothes on. She rips them off. Feral. I've got plenty of children, but this one can't be tamed. For five years I've troubled with her, but she's still no different from a wild dog."

"In a word, she won't answer when you call her?"

"Oh, no, ma'am, not at all."

The lady of the manor took out her papers, wrote at length on them, then had Mrs. Dudás sign them.

"I'm instructing you, Mrs. Dudás, to bring the child tomorrow morning at nine o'clock. I advise you until then to lock her in the house, don't let her out before then! I don't want people chasing after her across the puszta. In short, bring her tomorrow morning without fail, and hand Orphalina over to Miss Margit, my assistant."

With that she got up, packed her bag, and closed it.

"Orphalina State. That's her name. Pretty stupid name. No doubt Secretary Kiséry gave it to her."

And as she exited through the door:

"As far as she's concerned quite fitting. The secretary is very compassionate. To be truthful, I didn't know that was her name, that she had no other. I'm just seeing it now from the documents."

"God damn it!" the fragile woman cursed once the lady of the manor had left, "just when we might get some real use out of her, you go and take her away."

She went out to the back of the yard and yelled:

"Chick-Chick, Chick-Chick, the devil take you, Chick-Chick."

"So what does she want?"

"Come, she already left."

Chick-Chick saw that the lady of the manor had gone, but she was still afraid she'd come back if she went inside.

"She'll come back."

"No she won't. And I'm going away, too. Come when I tell you to, or I'll break your neck, don't make me mad. Come now, child."

She gently coaxed the little girl over to her, but Chick-Chick refused to go inside, instead observing from without how mama dear put on a black dress, tied a black-and-white dotted scarf on her head, and she found it so strange – mother only looked like that when she occasionally went into the village to shop.

"You shopping?"

"What's the matter?"

"You shopping?"

"Yes, because of you I have to go to the village, damn their hides, all of them, those gentlefolk, all they do is screw us poor people over. Because of you I have to go, you pest. All because of you. For the school I have to go all that way."

Chick-Chick couldn't understand why mama dear had to go to school because of her.

"Until I get back, you can clean. You can wash. But if you break anything, I'll stand on your legs and rip you in two."

Chick-Chick's eyes opened wide: she could wash up? What happiness.

Oh, how splendid it was. She warmed some water, poured it into the tub, started washing the dishes one by one, of which there were a great many, all of them dirty, unwashed, as mama dear didn't like doing that, she never got to it, she only washed now and again when she was able to conjure up the time. Little Chick-Chick, how she loved splashing around in the tepid water, what a tremendous feeling to be allowed to handle these fragile objects by herself. At other times not a one of them comes into her hands, she has a tin dish like dogs use, she has to eat from that, from a scratched, dented, unwashed tin dish, so that she won't break any pottery or porcelain. Now she alone is lord in the big house, no one is there but her, saving Marci, the shiftless old black cat, who sits there on the oven, purring if she feels like it, and the white dog outside, and the pigs, and Borisa, and the hens, the rooster, and the cheeky sparrows, who constantly flutter about the porch, or fly down onto the threshold into the kitchen, even though a table is laid for them out there now, across the entire field.

They are all pecking and picking for themselves, she is the only one working in this world.

Once she's dried off a dish, she would have to put it up on the plate rack, in the front room, over the chest of drawers, but she can't reach it. But she has a solution. She looks for a milking stool, places it in front of the chest, and in this way she is able to store the porcelain platter, and everything, the cups, jugs, salt cellar.

After that she tidies up the kitchen, putting everything in its place, rinses out the tub like mama dear does, sets it in the corner beneath the ladder, and as they still haven't come home yet, she sets to work in the front room. In the main house, where she isn't allowed to go. Now it's all hers, she'll do with it as she likes. She takes the broom and sweeps out every nook and cranny, she even removes the sweepings from the house, throws them into the wind, the wind merrily carries the laughing dust particles off into the sunlight.

But now she thinks up a truly ambitious task: she'll refinish the entire floor.

She retrieves mud from the heap behind the house, adds water to it, looks for some soot to put in it, and mixes it with her hands. It has to be nice and smooth, so that the handstrokes will disappear when it's spread on the floor. She never attempted to mud the floor before, but she looked on as mama dear did it; and now with her little hands and a smoothing rag she starts working, from one end to the other. It has to end up looking as though it were finished with boards, or were made of glass, smooth and of a single hue; the little girl who squats there naked on the floor bears a remarkably attentive expression, all dedication and diligence. She works as busily as a little fairy, a grimy, black fairy, in place of clothes she's clad in mud, her entire body is splattered in a coating of black liquid, her knees are black, her feet, her legs, her entire belly, even her face, her plump little biscuit of a face resembles that of a chimney sweep.

But she doesn't look at herself, she just moves ahead with her work, eagerly; she's finished by the time her siblings arrive back home from school.

"You can't come in here," she shouts at them, "you can't come in here. I mudded the floor."

"Who, you?"

The bigger ones snigger, and Rózsi even sticks out her tongue.

"That's right, me."

That is seriously funny to think she's refinished the floor, when their mother didn't even let the eldest of them, Zsófi, do that job.

But they don't go in, as they can see that it's wet, they go in search of something to eat, and find what they were looking for. Chick-Chick hadn't touched a thing, she didn't eat a single bite all day, not daring to eat, only to work, even fearing as she was working that she'll get it if she doesn't do it well, and she'd really get it if she ate something up that isn't meant for her.

Only if they give it to her. But it doesn't occur to her sisters to offer anything to her, so she stands there as black as pitch, like a muddy piglet, looking on at them with her face beaming, happy and proud, she laughs and laughs with her little mouse teeth, everyone who looks at her is seized with laughter, it's too comical to see how she herself is coated in mud.

"Go wash yourself, you pig," Jóska cackles at her.

"I will."

She goes out to the well, stands in the trough, and there she washes herself from head to foot, awkwardly, but with dedication, until she's scrubbed the last bit of mud from her feet. Nonetheless her feet remain black, as does her entire body, as she hasn't gotten any soap to wash with, her skin is tanned black.

"Who washed the dishes? Who was that good girl of mine?" mama dear asks, as she immediately notices upon entering, even in the darkened room, that the plate rack above the chest of drawers is full to the brim with clean dishes, just not as she is accustomed, they have a completely different arrangement.

But now for once she smiles, her queer mouth emerges from its eternal sadness and draws itself into a smile.

Chick-Chick just stands out there in the kitchen next to the door, casting a shy glance inside, waiting to see if mama dear will notice her, and behold:

"Chick-Chick."

"Chick-Chick? I thought you all had done this when you'd gotten home from school, but you wretches, you never help your mother out."

She paid no mind to anything else. She took off her scarf and placed it in the drawer. She took off her black dress and put it in the armoire. Then she put on her accustomed, worn-out blue dress, and left the room.

"What happened with this scrubbing in here? Maybe you all peed there and the cat wallowed around in it," she laughed. Chick-Chick was waiting for her praise – she laughed too.

"What's up with this room, who in the heck messed it up?"

"Chick-Chick."

"What did that pig do with it? What did you do?"

But Chick-Chick proudly proclaimed:

"I mudded it."

"What the hell? You?"

Then she took a closer look. Even the cracks have been repaired, they're still soft to the touch, but skillfully smoothed, without flaw. And the mudding isn't bad for all that, it could probably stay just like it is. There's work enough outside, so for the sake alone of keeping up appearances, she growled:

"Oh, who in the heck said you could do that."

Only that evening, when she sat down for a bit and ate, she said:

"You ... did you eat? ... well, eat ..."

When she saw how cheerfully and voraciously the little girl started nibbling on her bread, she moaned:

"God should strike those people, taking her away from a person just when she could finally be of some use."

In the morning she sighed:

"Come here, then."

And the little girl flung herself onto her lap, nestled up against her and wrapped her small arms around her. That was all the reward she needed, just knowing mama dear loves her. And lets her snuggle up to her. Rest her head against her, press her face into her bosom, feel her pat and stroke her back, and mama says:

"I've got a nice little daughter here ... or would have ... if those wretches wouldn't rob her from me ... Come then."

Chick-Chick just looked at her mama dear. Why call her to her so early in the morning?

"Come on, I'm taking you in to the village, to the market."

To the village?

Chick-Chick gasped. Never in her life had she gone to the village. And mama dear is going to take her into the village. To the market.

What wonders are taking place today. Mama dear looks for a dress. A dress from Rózsi. She looks for a shirt and a smock.

"Come on, I'll get you washed up."

She pours warm water into the big washtub, stands the little girl in there, and washes her with soap. How nice that tepid, soapy water is, mama dear's hands, her rough, gnarled hands wash her much as she herself washed the dishes yesterday.

How strange, it tickles – she's never worn a shirt before. Then the smock. But as for the shoes, there are none, as Rózsi wore the shoes to school.

They left some time ago, maybe she and mother, too, are going to school. That's why mama dear was to the village yesterday, to arrange the school. Chick-Chick doesn't know much about what has to be done with that, since she hasn't yet eaten anything that people call "school," but she senses that yesterday's errand had something to do with today's.

She patters barefoot in the cold dirt alongside mama dear.

From time to time she asked something, but didn't receive an answer, only a grunt, or a jerk that threatened to wrench her fragile little arm from its socket.

Then suddenly she got terribly thirsty. "Mama dear, I'm thirsty, mama dear, I'm thirsty."

"The devil take you, why didn't you drink something at home. Where am I gonna get water for you here?"

But Chick-Chick didn't care, she just said, over and over again, I'm thirsty, mama dear, I'm thirsty, mama dear, can't you hear me, I'm thirsty.

"We're coming up on the village well, you'll get some there."

But that was still a ways off. Nevertheless, they would get there eventually, which they did. Once arrived, mama dear led her to the well, cast a glance at the bucket, and as a little water was still in the bottom, she didn't have to draw more. Well, drink then.

The village was like something that couldn't be real. She'd never before seen such a quantity of houses, one beside the other. Out on the puszta there were no houses but theirs, Kadarcs's, and off in the distance one could see a house here, a house there, but here with row after row of houses, she thought her eyes would jump from their sockets, you couldn't tell one from the other.

"We're not going to the lady of the manor, but to her assistant."

She didn't know they had to see the lady of the manor, nor that the lady of the manor had an assistant, she merely recoiled in fright.

They entered a large house, the path to which was constructed of brick, but the bricks were laid such that it was pleasant to walk along them, each one was set a bit lower than the other, and their edges were rounded off.

Then mama dear led her through a great door, from which they stepped into some kind of fancy salon. But she didn't allow her eyes to wander, she pressed herself against mama dear's skirt and peeked out from there.

"I brought the child, miss."

"So you brought her, Mrs. Dudás? You're Mrs. Dudás, right?"

"Yes, I am, miss."

"I see. In that case you may go, the little one stays here."

But upon hearing these words, Chick-Chick took hold of mama dear's skirt with both hands, all but pulling it off, and leered anxiously, her mouth twisted, in the face of unknown danger; when the pretty, young, round-faced gentlewoman stood and approached her, she began to yell as though a knife were being thrust in her throat and she was about to be slaughtered and brined.

This startled the little gentlewoman, as well as mama dear.

"Don't cry, my child," and mama dear raised her apron so as to wipe the screaming child's nose and mouth, while at the same time concealing her from the frightened young lady. She just laughed and said:

"Don't cry now, sweetheart, little angel, dear child, my little dove."

But Chick-Chick screamed all the louder; she sensed that mama dear was afraid too, that she wasn't the same as at other times, not once did she say the hell with you, may your flesh rot from your bones, or that sort of thing, rather she terrified her with: sweetheart, dear child, my little dove.

The little gentlewoman ran into the other room and got a big doll from there. It was a doll with real hair, just like a small child, and it so frightened the child from the puszta that she ceased crying and stared at this strange animal: she'd never had a doll and couldn't imagine what sort of a thing this was, was it perhaps a schoolgirl? or what? like what they wanted to make out of her. For this reason, when the gentlewoman merely approached her with the doll, she started bellowing so dreadfully that the two women were afraid she was having a seizure.

She didn't even notice when mama dear left. Nor did she know that she'd let go of her hand and her skirt; suddenly she was just standing in the middle of the room, covering her eyes with her hands, sobbing, and when she looked around, no one was there but the pretty little gentlelady, as she'd noticed even in the midst of her crying that she'd never seen anything so lovely in her life, this strange gentlewoman was so kind and beautiful.

"Come here, my child. Little Orphalina, don't be afraid of me. You know, Orphalina, you're as pretty as the prettiest flower in spring, as pretty as a pansy you are, come now, come here to me, little Orphalina."

"I'm not Orphalina."

The gentlewoman was glad to hear her speak, she was thrilled to have calmed her down to that point.

"Then who are you?"

The question met with prolonged silence.

A dozen times she had to pose the question to her: who are you, when finally the girl blurted out:

"Chick-Chick."

"What?"

"Chick-Chick."

"No, your name is Orphalina. Orphalina State. That's how your name is entered, you are little Orphalina State."

But the girl furrowed her small brow, she sulked and looked around her spitefully, only now did she see that they were no longer in the same room where they'd been, but in the other room, where all the dolls were.

Everything else was just a blur.

She remained contrary and obstinate, gave no further answers, refused to be laid down on the pretty sofa, sensing that with her filthy feet it was not all right to lie down on the divan like the other little girls who lay there silent, some of whom were no bigger than a grown person's hand, and she was horribly afraid of them, she feared they would claw her, she didn't want to stay with them, for if the gentlewoman left, they would run at her, as regardless of how small they were, there were many of them, and what were their insides even made of?

Then she clenched her teeth, allowed herself to be laid down and tucked in, pretended and closed her eyes so tight that her eyeballs all but shifted from their spots, so that they thought she was fast asleep and the gentlewoman left her there, and when she was alone among the mute beings there, she raised herself up, then she snatched one of them like the cat snatches the mouse, and it didn't cry, it didn't even speak, and she recognized that those children weren't even alive, they were fake somehow, she tore the head off, and no blood came out.

She grabbed a second and a third, broke them, threw their heads against the wall, and saw that their heads were made of porcelain.

Who left the door open?

She fled from there, ran outside, ran along the street, looking back a few times, then she ran on, she ran so hard that she was almost out of breath, but she didn't dare stop, as she sensed that the ghosts were at her back: those porcelain-headed ghosts, dressed in white sheets, chasing her, she ran and ran along the street, on occasion a woman or a child or a dog gazed after her, but no one bothered with her, no one asked where she was going, she just went and went, as they were after her.

It was already completely dark, the village was far behind her, the countryside was beginning to seem familiar, as though she'd been at this very place with Borisa once – this wasn't their path, but it was just like it, and she went along breathlessly, hungrily, and dreadfully tired, she walked in the autumn night, she walked until she once again reached a village, and it shocked her that she'd kept going and going, yet she arrived again in the village, as she had no idea that there were two villages in the world, she'd never once heard that: she'd only heard "village," they'd always said: "to the village."

But here the dogs were brazen, once she had to scream, as from a gate two enormous dogs rushed out and stopped in front of her, and they barked their heads off: she didn't know that the dogs were barking not because they wanted to eat her, but because their hearts were broken over what a little Orphalina State such as her might be doing on the streets so hungry and tired, was she lost?

"Whose child are you?"

A strong, thickset woman came out from the yard, and asked once more in a loud voice:

"Whose child are you?"

"I'm afraid," the little girl answered.

"How did you get here?"

"Mama dear's gone."

"Where did you lose her?" And the woman bent down to her, and looked attentively into her face.

But Orphalina didn't dare tell the truth. She dared not say what she knew, instead she said:

"At the market."

"Where?"

"At the market."

"Who's your mother, then?"

"She is."

"Oh goodness, child, how dumb you are. Are you already in school?"

"In what?"

"In what, in what? She's the size of a schoolgirl, but as dumb as a four-year-old. Come on out."

She shouted this last across the yard, and a tall man in boots soon came out to the street.

"Look at this stray child. Who could be her mother? She was left at the market. When was the market?"

She took hold of the little girl, who wasn't the least bit afraid of her.

Not only was she not afraid, she spontaneously took off across the yard. The grown-ups merely watched to see what she was after.

The girl saw that this house was just like her own. Not like the one the lady of the manor lived in, but just like at home, there were the eaves, beneath that the bedstead, and the pigsty was there against the stable wall; the dungheap was near the well, the bucket swaying.

The grown-ups just watched and waited to see what would happen.

But the little girl merely stood there.

"Don't they live here anymore?"

"Who?"

"Papa dear and mama dear."

They laughed at this, the big man and the big lady.

"Come here my child, can you tell us what your parents' names are? Szekeres, Kovács, Bálint?"

But the little girl just shook her head; their nonsense only angered her.

"Dudás."

At this the two of them released a lively cry, the man as well as the woman:

"Dudás?"

"Of course, this is their state child! How in hell did she end up over here?"

Chick-Chick began to feel at home: the word "state," that was right too, the lady of the manor had said that, and at home they said that when they were very angry: state. She began to pluck up her courage since she was no longer lost.

"Come on inside, my child, I'll wash you up, you're all right now. Are you hungry?"

"I didn't eat anything today."

"You haven't eaten?" the auntie quipped amiably.

"'Cause mama dear said you don't get anything to eat here anymore, 'cause you're not working for us. They'll give you food where you're going to."

"Ah ... that Rozi, she always was a lousy pinchpenny. Look here, have a little bread."

She bit into it immediately and ate while she waited for the auntie to prepare water in the basin to wash her with. But that was taking so long that meanwhile she just sat there in the corner; the adults didn't bother with her, she just heard how they kept bad-mouthing the Dudáses.

"Say, that's that little naked girl," the man said suddenly.

He said it when she was already standing in the basin and the woman was washing her.

At that, she recognized them, these were those relatives, she'd once called this man uncle relative.

But she didn't dare look over at him, as it came to her attention that this uncle relative was looking at her like papa dear did, and Pista Kadarcs did, and the others. She turned her back to him and didn't look at him.

"Well, here's some nice, fresh, warm milk, it's still frothy," the woman said.

"Don't want any."

"Why not? Don't you like milk?"

"Don't want any."

"What'll you eat then?"

She didn't respond.

The next morning she woke up fit and healthy. It made her very happy to wake up in such a clean, pretty, white bed. She longed to go home. She longed for mama dear's pleasant, familiar odor.

For breakfast she got buttered bread. The woman even put some jam on it.

Then they hitched up the wagon, the two of them climbed into their seats and sat her down between them.

The wagon drove a long, long ways. They went clear across the village and then onward, onward, until suddenly the little girl just started crowing happily. The world began to open up before her as though her eyes were finally really seeing it. The trees she'd seen until now were just trees, the houses merely houses; but within the blink of an eye she was home, without realizing how she'd gotten there – there was the crooked acacia tree, and there was Borisa, tied to it.

"Where did you leave this child at?"

"Oh, hell, damn your hide, what are you coming back for? May the devil take your sorry soul, can't a person get rid of you?"

Chick-Chick laughed coyly, she was happy to be home hearing those precious words she'd heard her entire life long. She knows they're scolds and insults: but as long as they don't hurt. If these bring happiness, if these are what's good, and not that sweet talk that others bandy about ...

She was slithery enough not to show that she didn't miss a trick – if it applied to her, then she got it.

"I don't know what stuff she's made of," mama dear said of her, "blue-blooded or something, 'cause she's very sensitive, she's completely useless, thin-boned. She wouldn't be a bad child, she works hard, but she isn't good for anything, she's weak. You can't coddle a child like that, she'd turn into a little princess before you know it."

The next day the servant girl came out.

It was said she was the manor lady's maid. A big, strong girl, quick to laugh.

"I'll just take this little hooligan along," she said with a snicker. "Tie 'er up. She's gotta be tied up, I'll get 'er taken care of."

And she snorted with laughter.

And indeed, they got her dressed once again, then they fetched a piece of rope that Borisa had broken off, and bound her two little hands together with it, and the servant grabbed the end of the rope to draw her along with.

But the little girl was as white as a sheet and said:

"Let me go!"

She didn't let her go. She pulled her. She was strong, the girl had to go with her.

Mama dear was even smiling. She saw that the child was in strong hands. She wouldn't be coming back.

Then the little child lunged at the servant's hand and bit into it. She barely managed to tear the child away from her. But she merely laughed, she didn't get angry, didn't slap her.

In this way she led her by the rope, like a little calf to the slaughter.

Along the entire way the battle between them continued, the girl repeatedly lunged at her, repeatedly bit her.

At the village well, the jovial servant said:

"But why do you wanna stay with that nasty woman?"

"My mama dear!" the little girl screamed tirelessly.

"I've got news for you, you idiot: that's not your mother. She got money for keeping you. – They paid her, you dunce! She didn't love you. She only loved the money, not you. If she were your mama dear, then she wouldn't've let you go ..."

The little girl fell silent.

"Soon you'll get another mama dear, it'll be the same way, she'll take you 'cause they'll give her money for you. But maybe she won't be so godawful."

It seemed as though something had gotten into the child's little head.

"Everyone wants a state child. There are other state children besides you. For money anyone will be a state child's mama dear! Idiot."

She no longer needed to pull her with the rope.

The little orphan walked alongside the girl with head bent. She didn't understand it all, but something had grown cold inside her, and she no longer longed for her mama dear so much.

Fifth Psalm

The little girl peered intently at the strange lady; it amazed her to see that someone so young and apple-cheeked would want to take a state child. Until now she'd believed that a state child would only go to people who were old and shriveled, but this person still had such a plump, round face that a Sovari apple was neither firmer nor redder. Her hair was flaxen beneath her finely-spun scarf, her eyes were blue. But her voice rang as shrilly as if she were being sliced up with sedge, and she spoke haughtily:

"Well then, little girl, kiss the gentlewoman's hand and let us go, dusk is falling, and we've a ways to go yet."

She spoke oddly, as though she were inventing the words as she said them.

Meanwhile the little girl had worn herself out, she bent silently over the gentlewoman's hand: it wasn't like mama dear's hand, rather it was white and smelled of soap. She kissed it, and listened to all the good advice about the importance of behaving properly.

"You will be well placed here, my child, with Mrs. Szennyes, you'll be among wealthy people, you'll have nice clothes, food, everything will be good, you'll go nicely to school, you'll have books, you'll learn to write, to read, everything will be good, you must just be on your good behavior. Be sure to be on your best behavior, so that I don't hear anything bad about you. Don't take your clothes off, it isn't allowed to go about without clothes on, do you understand?"

"What the hell? She's been going around without clothes on?" Mári Zsaba asked, astonished.

The gentlewoman laughed off the unvarnished word "hell," but then she feared it would harm the child, so she amended her comment:

"Her previous foster mother complained – out of anger, I think, that the child would be taken from her – that she couldn't stand to have clothes on."

"That's nothing, ma'am – well, thank you, can I take the empty basket? Go into the kitchen, little girl, and get the basket."

Who knows what was in the basket and how it got into the kitchen, but one thing is certain, she took the big empty basket home, to a place where it had never been before.

Mári Zsaba had such a perky gait, she fully jiggled her big fat fanny right and left. When they'd left the village, they went along a broad road lined by trees, acacia trees looked down on them from either side; well, Orphalina thought to herself, this would be a fine place to graze Borisa. The grass was nice beneath them.

It didn't occur to her that this could soon happen.

No, that didn't occur to her, as she would soon be going to school, and she shuddered somewhat anxiously as she wondered what this school would be like that she'd heard so much about from the children, though she herself had never yet been there. But it was nice that she was to go to school, like going to a little piece of heaven. Armed with these thoughts, she happily bore the big basket, dragging it along beside the strange woman. She'd never seen such a woman from up close, she came across as so very aristocratic, it was impossible to imagine her working on the farmstead. Her plump little body filled every hollow of her elegant dressing gown. From front to back, in every direction, like melons in a sack. At last they came to a vineyard.

These aren't mama dear's anymore, these ought to be tasted.

"Auntie ... a grape or two would be nice ... I'll put them in the basket."

She added this last, as Mári Zsaba should get some too, she'd have to give her some.

"What in the hell are you thinking, you can't do that, the field keeper'll come and lock you up."

At this the little girl fell silent, while the big, plump, fulsome clusters of grapes looked out from the vines, snickering at her: "Well, little girl, you'd like some grapes? Hee-hee ..."

Before they'd passed the vineyard, Mári Zsaba said:

"Where are you running off to? We're already home."

It was a large farmyard, huge buildings stood before them, it struck the little girl as an entire village: was all of this Mári Zsaba's?

"So what's for dinner?"

Zsófi said:

"It's there on the bench by the stove."

But Zsófi said this so haughtily, as though she weren't even the servant, and looked angrily at the little state child.

"So, Lispy, this is yours," the woman said.

"I'm not Lispy."

"What are you then?"

"Orphalina, the manor lady called me Orphalina."

"And what did your mother call you?"

"Chick-Chick."

"That's what you are, you little lisper, you don't even know how to talk."

"'Cause nobody taught me how, but soon I'm gonna go ta s-school," Chick-Chick stammered, lisping, recognizing only now that she didn't speak properly, rather indistinctly, or with a lisp.

"Eat this."

It was dark in the kitchen. There was no way to know what was in the pot, she ate all the flies as well with which the sauce teemed, she thought they were crackling.

Mári Zsaba brought her into the little room where she herself slept, and showed her: "This is where you'll sleep, with me. Uncle Fere isn't home today, when he's home he doesn't sleep here, he sleeps outside with the cattle."

That was fine, since papa dear likewise always slept out in the stable, winter as well as summer.

Suddenly she heard Zsófi say:

"She's not choosy, she eats the flies, too."

And she laughed about it.

She was exhausted from the change in homes and fell asleep right away. But all of a sudden she woke up when she understood what Zsófi had said, that she'd eaten the flies! That wasn't crackling? It was flies! She was overcome with such disgust at this that in that moment she became ill and began to vomit.

Mári Zsaba woke up:

"Hey, what in God's name is she doing there? Hey, what's going on? What are you doing to me?"

She lit the lamp and saw that everything, all the sauce the girl had inside her, was spewing out, up and down.

"Oh, you nasty beast, you're not sleeping with me anymore, you filthy beast, you've made a mess of my bed."

With that she took hold of her and threw her out of her room, then shouted at Zsófi to take her away.

"Look what she did to my bed, you beast, eat it, choke it down. Zsofka, from now on she sleeps with you, the beast, she won't set foot in my room ever again."

Zsófi likewise touched the little girl as though she was immediately going to bite or infect her, she suddenly appeared frightful to the big, corpulent adult, a monster she must fear.

"I told you she was full of flies," Zsofka mumbled, "she threw up nothing but flies."

The next morning, while she was still dead asleep, they woke her up at three in the morning and sent her out to accompany the pigs to the field.

There she loafed about on the stubblefield until noon – she didn't feel like singing.

The neighbor's swineherd joined her then, he too was a youngster, but he could have been eighteen years old.

"So, Mári Zsaba went into town, she'll tell the manor lady that I made a mess of her bed, but I'm leaving too, I'm not sticking around here to eat flies; watch after her pigs, I'm going home to mama dear."

With that she took off, at the end of the stubblefield the woods began, she went into the woods, and walked and walked ever farther into the forest. She lingered at length beneath the trees, the woods were dense, one could see nothing but the treetops, where there was likewise nothing worth seeing. The undergrowth made going onward impossible; she found a colorful mushroom, tasted it, but immediately she sensed how it burned, she tossed it away, the small place where it had touched stung her tongue for some time.

At noon she turned back and went the way she'd come, as she had no idea which way to go in the big forest.

"So you came back?" the little swineherd asked her.

"Yeah, 'cause I didn't see anything."

In that moment, Zsofka brought lunch.

"Here, you piece of filth," she said, and she thrust it at her as though they were mortal enemies. "Where will you sleep?"

"In Mári Zsaba's room."

"The hell you will, she won't put up with a puker like you."

"I never did it before, I just did it 'cause of the flies."

"Damn the flies, what flies."

When she went home that night, she slept with Zsofka, and she slept soundly, she didn't move a muscle until morning.

"You know, she didn't move a muscle all night long, she slept like a log."

"The devil eat her innards, then it was just those flies that turned her stomach. What a namby-pamby. Even a state child gets squeamish and finnicky. Here's the milk, drink it."

"Don't want any."

"What don't you want?"

"Milk."

"Look at that, what'll it be next? I'm not slaving away for this beast. What the hell – you won't drink the milk?"

"No."

"Why not?"

"'Cause I don't like it."

"You don't like it, the devil should have taken you before I ever laid eyes on you, I didn't bring you here for you to like or not like my food, just go, take the pigs out. If you don't drink it, it'll stay here."

"I'm going to s-school."

"Where in the world?"

"To s-school."

"The hell you're going to school. Take the pigs out."

❀

The washing was ready, which Mári Zsaba dearly loved to do, that you had to get used to, for here there was no end to the washing and scrubbing that had to be done.

"I'd sooner do the washing ten times over than bake bread even once."

The little girl just stood around with the pigs.

"Come here."

She dunked the girl's head in the lye and washed it thoroughly, without soap.

"That won't hurt you. It won't hurt you a bit."

The little girl screamed.

Back in those days it wasn't even lye, but rather caustic potash.

"Now you can go. I'll soon cure you of your prissiness! Are you going to drink up the milk?"

"I'm not gonna."

"What an ass, and can't even talk right. Rinse off your head in the trough, then be on your way."

The stubblefield, the stubblefield, how beautiful is the wheat stubble.

Just like at the Dudás's, which is truly amazing – the Dudás farmstead is so very far away, and yet the grass blades there are just the same as the Szennyes's here. The cow is different, but she nibbles in just the same way, so the girl can enjoy the nice sound of her crunching and munching. Likewise she can sing here just the same, the thread of her melody echoes afar, and here as there the same notes sound forth from her mouth, so that there is no difference other than that here she no longer goes about naked, she's always clothed, in her state smock, and beneath that there is a shirt, too. Therefore it's better here.

Only during that brief time when she's at home, since now when she drives the cow home, she has to lead her across the large Szennyes yard, between two buildings, into the stable, a large, clean building, which the old man maintains, but at the Dudás's she would have to muck out the stable were she able to. And she misses all the children, here it's quiet, only Mári Zsaba's voice is heard, when she curses about this or that.

And even on Sundays she has to drive out the cow, for the cow wants to eat on Sundays, too. The poor thing is milked on Sundays, so as they take her milk on Sundays, she can't go hungry just because it's the Lord's day.

The day grows on, ever later, this lovely Sunday, then she sees a great sight: Mári Zsaba is coming.

Oh my, mama dear never brought dinner out to her, not even on Sunday, she'd had to make due with whatever she'd brought with her in the morning, so it really is better here. When she left in the morning, the scent of meat broth had reached the little girl's nostrils, she could already taste the meat broth, and the carrots cooked with it, she adored those. She began to skip, to dance, to cheer, for if she got some, she'd erupt into a frenzy of joy: here is the nice Sunday meat broth!

Mári Zsaba arrives, she greets her pleasantly:

"Good day, little girl, little Lispy," and she sits down on the thick grass, she isn't much for walking, she prefers to sit.

Lispy just looks at her in wonder, directing a suspicious stare at her.

"Come here, little girl, I've brought you dinner. Lispy."

But Lispy sniffs in vain, no pleasant aroma rises to her nose. Mári Zsaba now undoes the cloth, the lovely white cloth with a red stripe woven along the edges, and she takes out a plump little jug. What could be inside it?

She also takes out some white bread, not a large piece, but still, it's white.

Soured milk was in the jug.

The little girl says nothing, she doesn't complain, she lowers her head. She can have that too, the soured milk, it doesn't repulse her like the stinky fresh cow's milk, but it could just as easily be meat broth.

"Well, how are you?" Mári Zsaba asks her.

But she merely shrugs her shoulders, without answering, she doesn't even know what to say, and says nothing. She eats, picking at the nice white soured milk, it's like goose fat, just as greasy, mushy, and white, not something she likes, such fat.

"Are you happy with me? Do you like it with me? Just look, like peony petals in summer. Do you like me?"

"Sure, I like you."

"You no longer wish you could go back to your mama dear?"

"Of course I'd like to go back to her."

"To hell with you, you're not going back there anymore, here it's better for you, no one hurts you, right, you've got it good, right, no one hurts you?"

"There aren't so many flies anymore."

Mári Zsaba laughed. Yes, she'd eaten those. She laughed some more. What else does she want?

"So the cow doesn't vex you? If the flies plague her, just grab the rope, don't let her run off."

But she just sits, and the little girl repeatedly squints at her from a distance, distrustfully – today is Sunday, maybe she's brought some sort of pasta dish along? Today they're having cheese blintzes, this morning she mixed the parsley in with the cheese curds. But it isn't showing up now.

And once Mári Zsaba has had a good rest, she just reaches for the little girl, draws her towards her, hugs her, then gets up and leaves.

"God be with you, my child."

But Chick-Chick looked after her, hanging her head, and said to herself: you hugged me because you didn't bring me any meat broth.

It's no longer possible to lie in the grass for days on end, as even though the sun is shining, the ground is cold, and it hasn't been long since it rained, it still isn't dry. A cowherd must always be on her feet, walking and watching as the cow tirelessly chews the grass. She stretches out her big, black tongue, using it to shovel the grass blades into her dark mouth.

❀

"So, did you get her home?"

But the little girl is angry. All day long she thought about the meat broth, now she sulks, she's been cheated, and she mutters with darkened face:

"Of course I got her home, what do you think, like I'm gonna watch your cow for you at night."

My, how Mári Zsaba gapes at her.

"What the hell did you say?"

"There was meat broth for dinner," the little girl accused her, "with carrots in it too."

Mári Zsaba's two round, red cheeks grew pale with amazement.

"You didn't give me any," said the little girl.

What an outrage for the brat to talk to her like that. Just wait, but Ferenc Szennyes heard it, and he stepped from out of the dark of the portico.

"What's this, you didn't give this child any of the meat broth? And you bragged about how you brought her dinner."

"I did, too, what are you poking your nose in it for? She got plenty, she's not going to die on my watch. She got a jug full of soured milk, and white bread. I'm not going to spill the meat broth bringing it all that way."

"But damn it all," Ferenc Szennyes shouted, "I won't tolerate your cheating the child. The neighbors will get wind of it, and tell everyone that she doesn't even get a decent meal on Sundays."

They fought like dogs, soon they were both shouting at the top of their lungs, wielding their voices like the herdsmen did their whips. And Mári Zsaba turns then, goes into the kitchen to fetch a nice piece of meat, cooked meat from the soup, on an earthenware plate, and a vegetable dish, she fetches that too.

"See, there was meat broth!" Chick-Chick says. "That's what that's from."

"May the devil slap your stinking little mug, you brat – she saw it before."

But the little girl just laughs to herself: she eats up all the meat and the side dish. Then she sings.

"March off to bed!"

Cheerfully she goes into the servant's room, washes her feet with the water in the basin, singing out loud all the while:

one hump, two humps ...

She's very happy to have gotten some meat broth after all.

When the little girl returned home from the pasture the following evening, the woman was two people. She'd given birth to a child. That's why she was as plump as a stuffed pillow.

But even from her bed she fussed about the state child:

"Oh, what have I gotten myself into, breaking my back running after this one," she cried. "I thought, I'll take a little kid, it'll grow up, and I've got a little nanny for my own child. But she's worthless, this glutton is good for nothing. Thus God has struck me down."

The little girl only now heard the voice of the farmer:

"Just look after yourself. You've got enough to worry about. Still you waste your breath badmouthing that little state child. Just be glad you've got a child of your own now."

The girl stood outside the door, she put her fingers in her mouth, she saw now that she'd landed in a bad place; her heart broke as she thought of mama dear, she still couldn't believe that poor, sickly woman wasn't her real mother ... Or would this woman become her mama dear, now that she'd entered motherhood?

Sixth Psalm

The old man lived in the stable, he never came out of there unless work demanded it, but as soon as he could he withdrew back inside again.

"That was her uncle," Zsofka told the little girl with a snicker one evening as she climbed into bed alongside her. She used to tell her then:

"Those people don't pay anyone, believe me, they're wealthy – wealthy people don't pay their workers. They don't pay me either, I don't know why I'm such a fool, breaking my back for them. He was a weaver. The old man was. He just went bankrupt. Had a big house. Oh, how they carted the thread to him, he worked day and night, yet still he was ruined and ended up here; he'll never amount to anything anymore, they took all his land from him to look after him in his old age, but they don't even give him anything to eat, he cooks for himself there by the dungheap, and does nothing but work, work, work."

Whenever someone told her stories, the little girl felt she had a story to tell, too. She just said whatever came to her mind:

"The cellar was way at the back of the house. One time mama dear didn't hide the key and papa dear s-saw it, he took it then and went into the cellar, then he poked a hole in the bottle gourd, then he took s-some wine out, then he got a round belly just like Borisa, then Borisa's belly was as big as a keg, then when he came up out of the c-cellar, he grabbed the knife, then he s-said: 'I'm gonna end you all, now I'm gonna end you,' then we took off for the haystack ..."

Zsofka listened, she stared at the little girl who'd never opened her mouth in front of her before, but didn't understand what she was talking about. She'd never spoken to her until now.

The servant was a little curious, but as she couldn't make out what the girl was saying, she thrust herself over so hard that the bed almost fell in on itself:

"Oh, the devil take you, let's go to sleep, we'll soon have to get up again."

As little as she was, the little girl understood that here she was with a different kind of people from the ones at mama dear's.

Here the farmers are fat and the animals are fat. For the cows, horses, hens, all of them, they put out great quantities of feed, as they were always calculating their worth, how much they have to put into them in order to get a good price out of them. At Dudás's everyone was skinny, the husband, the wife, the kids too, and the animals too. Everyone went about barefoot, thus the nails on Papa Dudás's big black toes were split just like the horses' when their hooves broke off. And Mrs. Dudás never put on slippers, it would have had to be awfully cold for her to put her feet in another creature's hide. There was only one resemblance: here she was no more allowed to talk than there.

But this Mári Zsaba, she wore shoes, she wore stockings, and she always had on a clean dressing gown, especially since she had the child. The husband, Ferenc Szennyes, went about in sport shoes, not boots and short pants like the true noblemen. And he always had a cap on his head, cocked off to one side.

Here they weren't stingy with anything, except the employees. The old weaver, the uncle, was permitted only to take raw potatoes from the pit, they didn't give him any cooked food, he had to get by on basically nothing, and they begrudged him even that. Zsofka ate whatever she could get, but she often scolded Mári Zsaba, who kept all the keys on her and would likely carry them into her grave. So it seemed she didn't have access to everything either, but Chick-Chick noticed that the wife hid the nicer foods, and the pastries, in the parlor, so that none of them would even lay eyes on them. These they ate themselves, especially the apples. The fruit. As long as this was on the tree, not so much as a bud could be plucked, for example behind the house there was a white plum tree, she would have dearly loved to taste its fruit, but God forbid, they would probably have cut it out of her if there'd been a single shriveled fruit inside her, nor was it permitted to go anywhere near the tree. And they took all of it to the market, every bit, always to the market. Then once the tree had been picked, leaving only shriveled remnants, at that point climbing the tree was allowed, but the old man called the little girl over and told her, don't eat that shriveled fruit, or she would get sick, as it was affected by brown rot.

Whoever worked for them and could not be sold off also got nothing to eat. There was a big dog there, it didn't get anything either. It was such a large, skinny dog, always traipsing around sadly; little Chick-Chick felt sorry for him and often gave him a little bread. Once she brought out her soup to him, which Mári Zsaba saw – a huge ruckus ensued, she cursed like the devil, so bitterly that even the child cringed, although she wasn't exactly coddled, since the Hungarians from the plains knew no other way of speaking in those days than by using obscenities.

One time she saw the manor lady from afar. She was watching the piglets at the time, and the manor lady could see her as well, that she was there barefoot among the piglets in the cold mud, but she didn't call her over to her, she only spoke to Mári Zsaba.

Surely she's asking now whether I'm going to school, the little girl thought to herself.

In the afternoon when they called her in to eat, auntie Mári even said:

"Well, your gentlewoman was here, she asked whether you're being good."

"What did you say?"

"That you're being good."

The little girl was no longer so open and talkative as she'd been at the Dudás's, where she'd spoken to her foster mother like the other children did. Here she could no longer be intimate, here she was the same as an alien servant.

"What else did she ask?"

"Nothing. Whether you're learning well."

"I'm not even going to school."

"You'll go soon, don't worry. In any case you're too late. You'll go next year."

And soon after that she sent the girl to school. She had to go there with a basket, the basket held curd cheese, and she carried a couple of nice chickens under her arms. The teacher took the chickens and the curd cheese, said to send her regards to auntie Szennyes, and allowed the child to come into the school for a bit. She saw all the children, but looked in vain for the Dudás kids.

She didn't set foot in the school again that year.

But when the second year passed and it was again September, Mári Zsaba once again sent her to the teacher with a basket, and this time too she brought a couple of nice chickens, but it wasn't curd cheese that was in the basket, but rather eggs, lots of eggs, fifty of them.

And in this year they didn't send her to school either. She was already eight years old, and still they didn't let her go to school. While the other children were already in the third grade, she was grazing the animals outdoors, but the wheat was already growing up, so she couldn't take them out to the fields, but only beneath the acacia trees, she stayed there at the side of the road all day long; she was clothed, but barefoot. She wore a long state smock, but no shoes yet, they didn't give those to her yet, because the gentlewoman only gave them one pair, causing Mári Zsaba to complain bitterly that she stole the summer shoes, forcing them to save this pair for later, as otherwise she would have none for the winter.

It didn't occur to her that the earth wouldn't swallow her whole if perhaps she herself bought a pair of shoes for this little girl.

"Where in the hell were you?"

"Out, I wanted to go out to my mama, but I didn't find her."

Mári Zsaba looks at her.

"This brat's trying to find its mother."

Every day you had to rise before dawn if you wanted to survive on the farmstead. The grass was covered with frost.

"Here are Zsofka's slippers, go, run after the turkeys."

Chick-Chick cheerfully takes the slippers and runs off in them. The slippers are big, she trips in them, she has to go into the wheat as suddenly the turkeys are there, she forgets the slippers, only remembering them once she's restored the turkeys to their proper place. The slippers are gone.

Oh no! In tears she looks for them, she keeps looking for them all morning long, she found one, then lost it again.

"Just wait, you dog, no dinner for you!"

She can't find them, she looks, but finds nothing. The woman shouts at her:

"Drive the pig out."

She had to drive the pig out, but got nothing to eat.

At this time of year the wheat had already sprouted. The other morning, when she took the turkeys to the usual spot, immediately she found the slippers, but she didn't put them on, rather she held them in her hand so that she wouldn't lose them again. This worked well too, it was a help, as she could throw them at the turkeys. Once she struck a turkey down with them; terrified, she took the poor turkey into her lap and nursed it until it was well again, but she picked up the slippers so she wouldn't lose them.

"Lispy, stoke the fire."

Mári Zsaba was always washing, the fire was constantly burning beneath the cauldron, and from morning till evening she shouted:

"Lispy, stoke the fire."

She had to leave the piglets and run, and the woman kept scolding her for not putting enough wood on the fire. She flew into a rage, and while the little girl was hunkered there before the wash-boiler it was easy to grab her, shake her by the hair and slap her. By this time she'd started beating her – until now she hadn't hurt her, but now that she had a child she'd become testier:

"Lispy, stoke the fire."

But Chick-Chick lost her temper, because Mári Zsaba hit her so hard across her head with the wash stick, and then across her back, that it nearly broke in two:

"I'm gonna go to your mother's and tell her that you're always beating me."

What a good idea that was, and the next day she did indeed take off, she went and went, until she reached Mári Zsaba's mother's house. Her mother's name was Polka Zsaba. Lame Polka Zsaba. For she limped a little, but she was an amiable woman.

"Truth be told, Polka Zsaba's girl beats me hard, she always beats me," Chick-Chick told her.

"What does she do, my child?"

"Beats me."

Lame Polka Zsaba then felt terribly sorry for the little girl, and she gave her something nice to eat, and didn't even send her home that evening. The next morning she looked after their pig, they had a black pig with many piglets, and she looked after them.

Mári Zsaba's family didn't live far from there, and the little girl sang the whole day long, she all but sang her lungs out, she sang so happily, like the birds in spring, as she thought she no longer had to go back there. But old Palya Zsaba was as curmudgeonly and as miserly as his daughter – he sent her out in the morning with the piglets, and now he sent word to his daughter that she should come and get the eater. There were paprika potatoes for lunch, these Chick-Chick found truly delicious, she would never forget how good they were, but she'd barely swallowed a bite, and who came over here? Mári Zsaba arrived:

"Come home, my child, finish your lunch, then come nicely home."

"She's eaten enough," old Palya Zsaba said.

The daughter also spoke nice words, but with an ugly look; she promptly grabbed the girl's hand and took her home. Along the way she said:

"Don't say anything to uncle Ferenc, or I'll beat you inside out." These were relatively kind words for her, about as if she'd said: Greetings.

As though here anyone would ever greet the other, would say good day, good evening – here no one ever wished the other good day or good evening, at best they said: praised be ...

When they arrived home, she drove the pigs out to the field, and that evening when she returned home with the pigs, uncle Ferenc wasn't at home, so she was beaten with the rolling pin: "Are you gonna run off again? don't get enough to eat here?"

Chick-Chick cried: "No, no no, I'll be good, just please forgive me, please don't hurt me, it hurts," but to herself she thought: what a stinking hag she is, tricks me, says stoke the fire, and I laughed, may she be cursed, always just stoke the fire. What would you say if I was Mári Zsaba, and I screamed at you, come stoke the fire? Lispy! ... Ugh ... and she stuck out her tongue.

But gradually there was more frost, and every morning the cow had to be grazed there along the road, at the end of the village beneath the acacia trees in the ditch. All kinds of people passed by there, and they said: the devil take that Mári Zsaba, she should come and graze the cow barefoot in the frost. For the little girl did not put the slippers on again, she didn't want to get in trouble again over them, so she just froze and froze, her heels were frozen. "She herself oughta come out and tend the cow and let the girl sleep instead of her lazing around under the covers." For indeed she was sleeping, of course that beast was sleeping. When it was milking time and Chick-Chick brought the cow home, that's when Mári Zsaba arose from her quilt-covered bed. The poor little girl felt her feet, and the old weaver said: "Be careful, my child, if your feet are wrecked during your childhood, that can't be reversed when you're grown."

It was a mere trifle that aroused her to anger: "You piece of filth, you pig, what the hell, you insolent bitch, how are you holding that broom? You can't even do that much with your seven years? She wants to go to school? It's not school she needs, it's a beating."

This time Ferenc Szennyes heard her, he said:

"Don't talk like that to that child."

So now it was he that she went after.

The old weaver says: "Come, my child, I'll take you to church."

Eastertime had come, Easter, the resurrection.

The little girl put down the broom. "Oh my God, I'll get to see the church from inside!" She always carried on like that when she received a gift, she squealed like a lizard.

"Go to hell, get out of my sight," said Mári Zsaba in true Easter spirit.

Chick-Chick ran merrily to the big tub, she stuck her feet in there and washed them.

But suddenly Mári Zsaba was overcome by the holy spirit, and she said:

"Come, then, I'll dress you up nice."

When she was dressing her, she asked:

"Are you happy?"

"Ooo, ooo, of course I'm happy!"

The old man took her hand and they went the long way toward the church, but Chick-Chick looked only at the churchgoers, all of them were wearing shoes – it had been a waste to wash her feet, they were covered with dust again. It was a beautiful, sunny Easter, she could no longer put on her old shoes, as every one of her toes poked out of them. They could have been repaired, but Mári Zsaba hadn't thought of that. How fortunate that the weather is fair, if the weather were bad, then the old man wouldn't be able to take the poor girl to church.

He took her straight up to the gallery, and Chick-Chick could see everything. Everything. She saw everything that the church was and what the people did there. She saw the priest and the mass and all the people and the eucharist and Christ's body with its wounds, and it struck her with wonder that such a great lord as Jesus Christ, who was the greatest king of all, the king of kings, should be stricken with such wounds, it was enough to make one cry, that she should complain even without a single wound, but she's not complaining, only quietly lamenting her suffering.

"How much longer is that ass gonna talk?" she asked the old uncle, and pointed at the priest. Old uncle tugged on her arm: "Don't talk so loudly and rudely."

She grew afraid and fell silent, she didn't know it was rude to call the man in the white robe an ass, what would old uncle say if she told him everything that Mári Zsaba was accustomed to calling her.

Suddenly all the people began to move, they headed out, and the two of them likewise descended from the gallery, but old uncle took her back once more to the gallery, and they watched and waited, and while they were waiting and looking at all the people, she felt her heart would burst from her great happiness, as she was the happiest person on earth, and she saw Mári Zsaba among the many people, she recognized her by her scarf, she even said out loud: "Look, it's Mári Zsaba, look."

"Quiet, you mustn't speak," but it was impossible not to recognize such a colorful plaid scarf.

After that she wanted to see uncle Jesus' wounds, and her old uncle took her there, and she got to kiss Jesus' coarse hands and face and wounds.

As they walked slowly down the road, she said:

"Dear old uncle, I'm a lot like Jesus, because the State gives me wounds on my hands and my behind, because the State gave me over to Mári Zsaba, so she could beat me."

"My child," the old man replied, "whoever has the State as his nursemaid should think twice whether he wants to be born. Why were you even brought into the world to be a burden to the State, you little fool."

The way was long for him, he sat down on a milestone to rest, and talked and talked to the little girl, not caring whether she understood him or not.

"You see, I've also entered my second childhood, I also came to rely on the State as my nursemaid, but the good nursemaid undressed me but good. You know, when the Romanians came in here, they bombed the village, the bombs set precisely my house on fire, 'cause I had a large house, the Red officers were in the front room there, so that's what they targeted. Six bombs burst through the streetside windows, the seventh was an incendiary bomb, that set the entire house on fire all at once, along with the stable and the shed, everything went up in flames. We couldn't put it out, 'cause the Romanians wouldn't let us, they didn't set it on fire so we could put it out."

He wiped his forehead and took a big, soft breath. Surely he was telling these things to the little girl because he, too, needed to disburden himself from his pain and sorrow, if only in front of a child.

"In this way my house burned down to the ground, on the third day the main beam in the middle of the big house was still burning. And the insurance company didn't pay a thing, I'd paid for the insurance for thirty-seven years, and they didn't give me one penny, 'cause they said they didn't pay for that kind of fire, as it was set intentionally. You know, child, the war was in the State's interest, so in truth the State should have compensated me for my loss, since in the parish no one's house burned down except for mine and two or three others. They didn't get any compensation either, but I, oh dear, I got such a punishment from the State, oh heavens ... Now, when they brought in the business tax, I didn't know it applied to me, I'm a weaver, I never had to keep account records, then one day a shopkeeper tells me, uncle Csomor, go up to the parish hall, there's trouble with the business tax. I go up to the parish hall and tell the notary: if you please, notary sir, does the business tax apply to me, too? The notary says to me: uncle Csomor, the controller is just here, ask him. Well, I go to the business tax controller and ask him, he says wait a moment, he'll make a report ... So he made the report and I calmly go home. A day or two later I meet the shopkeeper, as we two had become as poor as newlyweds, I didn't have so much as a pan or a table in my house, which I'd just managed to rebuild somehow, I always had to go to the shop, since I didn't have an apprentice either, for a long time now no apprentice has entered this trade, and my wife couldn't go there either, 'cause she was so frightened by the bombardments that from then on the poor thing lay ill in her bed. The shopkeeper asks what they said, I tell him they made a report. Oh my, he says, that's bad, 'cause there'll be a penalty, at least seventy thousand crowns ... Well I got very scared, so again I go to the parish hall, luckily the business tax controller is there again, I tell him, don't punish me, 'cause the fire and water already punished me, you know child, oh how could you know that, back in 1919 there was a big flood, it destroyed everything of mine, on the fields too, he says they won't punish me too harshly. Then it came out that they fined me a hundred and forty thousand crowns."

The old man was deeply affected by his own story. All the memories came flooding back to him. The little girl just stared at his face, which was as white as bleached linen, and his head always ached, his moustache was completely white, and he neither let it grow out nor shaved it off, he just trimmed it straight across, he nose wrinkled oddly upwards, his blue eyes were moist, teardrops quivered on his creased, red eyelids.

"But that's not all, the State then came up with even greater means against me. The trade license. 'Cause you know, my child, I was just as much of an orphan as you are, little one, I had neither a father nor a mother, instead an old weaver took me in, at the time he was the oldest man in the village, then for a long time I was the youngest, and now again I'm the oldest. Well, I successfully learned the trade and I practiced it for forty-six years, that way I obtained a little house and a little land, only in the flood the water wrecked my fields, and the bombing my house, so then in order to rebuild my house I had to sell the land, and I put the proceeds into building the house. In any case, what the State was seeking from me I couldn't produce. With the business tax, too, they said I had to pay everything from the very beginning of when I started earning, retroactively, and they reckoned that I'd earned three million a month, yet even when I worked as hard as possible I didn't earn even half that. 'Cause you know, child, every night till midnight I sat at the loom and worked, barely even getting up to eat. Now they said that if I didn't have a trade license, then I must have been a bungler from the very beginning, and I wasn't authorized to work my entire life long. That's what the State said ... I went to the district judge and said, do I have to give everything up? The district judge says, you don't have to give it up, but I have to have experts working. There aren't any more, district judge sir, no experts, I'm the last professionally trained weaver in the parish, there are two others here who aren't experts and who've started working, you can't want for me to learn from them. He says, there's another old master weaver in Abony. Well I know the one in Abony, the people from Abony come to me, saying they won't give their fine material to their weaver to have it ruined. And now I'm supposed to apprentice with him?"

Chick-Chick saw how the first tear now fell from the old man's eyes. All she did, given her inability to understand what the old-timer was saying with her small young mind, was cuddle up to him warmly, and she squeezed his hand and laid her head on his arm like a good little child.

"That's why I say, little girl, that whoever has the State for a nursemaid should think twice whether he wants to be born into this world, for the State seeks the good, but it has no voice, it needs an advocate, the State is powerful, but its hand does not caress; woe is he who lands in the hands of the bureaucrats, no good comes from them, only bother, vexation, and harm."

He lowered his head and sat there, stiffening to the point where it seemed he would no longer even move.

The little girl's heart swelled from sympathy, she would have loved to recount such fine, dreadful things as the old man, and she said:

"Papa dear always caress-ssed me."

The old man at first didn't pay attention to the little lisper, he couldn't even understand what she was saying.

"Not caress-ss: caress ... ss ... sss ... sss ..."

"Ss-ss-ss ... ss-ss ... sss ..."

"Like the wind blows: ss ... ss ..."

"Ss-ss-s ... sss ... sss ..."

The old man had already taught her like this before.

Then the child continued with her story, and the old man's eyes grew wide. Saliva rose between his gums, so overcome was he with horror. His blood flooded his pallid face, then left it again, his complexion waxed blue and green in turn over what the little girl was saying, then he stood up and said:

"Come with me."

The child goes when she's called to, they set out on the way back to the village, but they'd barely turned around when Mári Zsaba came along. And they stopped.

"Just look at these pigs, still loafing about out here." She shuffled along jovially, waddling on her sturdy, fat legs and swinging her fanny like a wasp, if the wasp could walk with its bulging belly turned backward, like a crab.

"What sort of outrageousness is this, you should have gotten home long ago. What were you thinking? Are the animals supposed to go hungry? Who's gonna clean out the dung? The devil take you, you old clod."

Ferenc Szennyes stood listening behind his wife. He wasn't one to add to his wife's words, though now Mári Zsaba was actually right, it had been foolish to let the old man go to church. As though the animals could just be left to their own devices for half a day.

Strangers were also walking along the road; Szennyes knew that his wife wasn't concerned whether someone heard her or not, so he didn't even bark at her: shut up. But there was enough of a sense of honor in him that at least he avoided augmenting his wife's bluster. The young, strong couple had already gone a ways ahead, and the old man and the child were still just standing there beside the milestone. The old man leaned forward and just stood and stood, as though he were having a stroke. His head swayed like a pendulum, nodding without cease, not wanting to stop.

"Filth," he said then. "Mr. and Mrs. Filth ..." Precisely what "szennyes" meant.

After that he again stood at length, as the passers-by disappeared off in the distance.

"It's getting colder, let's go home ... Don't worry, my child, no matter how hard things are for you, you're still young: you'll get through it. The young always persevere. A lot of things will happen to you yet, good ones too. I was also an orphan, like you, I didn't have a father or a mother, I had no one on this earth, but I also had the fortune that at that time yet the State didn't bother with little children, a little orphan only went to someone who wanted him, no one got paid to take him, keeping children didn't bring in money ... she's my own relation and has a very hard heart, no wonder she's well off, she's got everything, a wealthy person thinks only of how he can get money, more and more money; and how he can exercise his power. That's why she needs you, to be a little outside helper for her, 'cause they could keep servants, six of them if they wanted, but they'd have to pay them, but this way she gets a little money. She gets something from me as well, 'cause she claims I inherited something from her uncle, but that's not correct, since what I have I gathered all from my own earnings with my poor wife, the two of us together, and whatever would have been left from her uncle at that time was taken to the last penny by their parents, the Zsabas and the Marós and the Tunkas and the rest, so that I was left without so much as a roof over my head, then after I got married I slowly started to get back on my feet, 'cause I had a very good wife, she didn't even eat, she just laid everything by for our old days, we didn't think it would go to the State: boom, they swallowed everything we had left after the war, and now these good people said: come home to us, uncle, you can live with us till the end of your days, we'll even cultivate your fields. Yes, they're cultivating them now, but how am I doing – it's a wonder they let me leave the farm, I thought that, as long as I live, they'd never let me out past the gate again, for they're still possessed of the fear of God, such that if someone knew how they've played me, it could very well cost them ... But look here, two gendarmes are coming this way.

"I think they're coming home for dinner from another village, they've come a long way, they were on patrol, because of that they have a lot of walking to do, you see ..."

But he spoke so slowly that in the process of pronouncing the first word, he already forgot the next one.

"Please, gendarmes, if you would stop," he said, greeting them with great subservience, "I was just aiming to come to you, if you would allow me, kind sirs."

"Well, old man, what is it?"

"Just step away off of the street, my child. Go on ahead, the gendarmes won't hurt me, nor you, but I have something to tell them that isn't for a child's ears. What was the name of your papa dear?"

The little girl stood there distrustingly and gave them a hostile look. She moved halfway off the road, feeling strongly like a kick or a slap would greet her here, it would be wise to scurry off. But she was afraid to run away, nor did she know where she should run to or how to get home ...

"It sounded like Doodle or something like that, his name did. Dudás, right ... So if you please, gendarmes – go on now, my child ..."

The gendarmes listened to the old man's story in dismay, then they called the little girl over, and as she refused to come, one of them ran after her, grabbed her as she ran and dragged her back by the arm. The other gendarme, however, reached into his pocket and retrieved a piece of candy for the child, but she didn't dare take it.

"That's how she is, gendarmes, that's how she's been raised, she'll pick apple cores up off the road and eat them. Without being disgusted. And, poor thing, even what's been tossed on the dungheap is good enough for her. So far she's never had anyone to take care of her. She's always been at the mercy of cruel people."

"It would be best if you would be willing to come to the barracks so we can draw up a report."

"Certainly, honored sirs, I myself would come, I would dearly love to come, but I can't manage to walk anymore. I'll be glad if I only make it back home once more and die. But God has brought you this way, honored gendarmes, because it can't be that such godless and loathsome people live on this earth and even get money from the State to exploit a little orphaned child in this way, who has neither a father nor a mother, no one to protect her on this earth ... who can live ..."

The gendarmes saw how fragile the old man was, so they contented themselves with taking notes in a notebook, they would draw up an official report at home later, they said. The little girl just looked on and laughed. It began to flatter her that everyone was occupied solely with her, but she preferred to keep her distance, and from there she watched furtively how the one gendarme and then the other glanced over at her, and it pleased her.

"Everyone's just looking at me," she said, not knowing that she was saying it out of pride and coquettishness. After all she was accustomed to it, as since she was first able to think, all men always looked at her. There was no knowing why. And the things they asked, all their questioning, that aroused her to mere laughter as well. And to shoulder-shrugging, and winking, and smirking: regardless of how small the little girl was, she was nevertheless a girl; she sensed that there were things that were her business alone – if she wanted to share them, fine, if not, then not.

"Let's amble along, then," the old man said, and they set out, but having gotten absorbed in his own talk, he continued chattering in that peculiar, quiet manner: "Ferenc Szennyes is Ferenc Filth because he lets the little girl watch the cow barefoot on the field, 'cause he should be buying her shoes, 'cause the State doesn't provide them. 'Cause the child cleans, watches, works, washes, she does everything as best she can, it wouldn't kill him to offer up an old, small pair of shoes for her feet, to think he'd have to pay a swineherd-shepherd-boy seven or eight forints, along with food, top-boots or at least drawstring shoes, and he's saving all of that now, but then he says if it costs him extra, why take in a state child? Some people."

"What did you want with the gendarmes, you dog. Tell me, what did you want with the gendarmes, you cur?"

And one blow followed the other.

The little girl held her tiny, frail hands over her face, her head, but still couldn't protect herself with them, Mári Zsaba just kept hitting her. But she had no desire to wear herself out with the beating, so she looked for a stick and seized on the wash stick, whose acquaintance Lispy had made once already, the same one she'd gotten beaten with when she hadn't stoked the fire.

"You'll croak here at my feet if you don't say what you wanted with the gendarmes!"

"It wasn't me, it was uncle," the little girl screamed with bloodied lips, and that calmed Mári Zsaba down.

She'd clung obsessively to the thought that the little girl had complained and the gendarmes had seen her barefoot and had accosted her because of that, as from afar she and Szennyes had seen how they'd questioned the little girl. But it hadn't occurred to her before that the old man would go making complaints. Doubtless he'd told them about his fields and how they treated him, this thought caused her immediately to forget about the child, to hell with her, she went into the other room and looked into what should be done with the old codger. "Don't let flies on the baby," she shouted across to the little girl, who dutifully rushed to the cradle and shooed away the flies.

"Wah, wah," said the baby in the cradle, and he cried continuously. "No doubt he gets bad milk from his mom, as she's always so full of venom, her milk is venomous too," Zsofka remarks as she comes in from the front yard. "Bad milk is what she gives, that one, as she's just like a carbuncle. In this house everyone gets bad milk, 'cause everyone's in a bad mood from morning till night. And you know, even Mári Zsaba could be in a good mood if she wanted, since she never has to do anything but crochet all day for her baby. Her husband does all the work, such a little man, unbelievable, forever just working, he even enjoys doing the woman's work, the cooking too. He does Zsofka's work, too, if he's of a mind to, while the wife sits there in the front room with her crocheting, staring into space like a viper – if she'd only just stay in there." And the little girl, Lispy, just shooes the flies away, and when she hears Zsofka's soft laughter from the kitchen, how she laughs over the farmer, it occurs to her that in the summer when they were outside on the threshing floor, the wife had to go in the house, leaving the three of them there, her and Zsofka and the farmer on the canvas; the farmer says then, "shove Zsofka over this way." "Why?" she asks him, "maybe you wanna rub it in?"

She smiles now thinking of this, though also of the questions the gendarmes asked, things that people normally didn't ask.

So Mári Zsaba opens the door, her rosary around her neck. What's this, she wasn't crocheting in there, she was praying the Rosary?

Mári Zsaba looks at her brat, there's a fly on his face, maybe it's left over from the autumn as it's so lethargic, then it fell on him and couldn't crawl away anymore.

"This is how you look after my child? This is how you look after my child?" She undoes her rosary and takes it off, then starts beating the little girl's head with it.

"May God strike you dead, you shameless pig" – she just beats Chick-Chick's head like this, but as she can't get any blood to flow with the rosary, she removes the embroidered Szeged slipper from her foot and uses its wooden heel to pummel the child's head, hitting her with all her might: "That's how you look after my boy, you cur?"

She didn't stop until she'd cut the girl's head open.

Her blood flowed, Ferenc Szennyes was watching from the kitchen, wearing a big apron; he said:

"So is that what you went to church for?"

The blood dried in Chick-Chick's hair, and Mári Zsaba locked her up in the servants' room, but that evening she called her out and pressed a mug into her hand.

"Take this to that other beast, to your friend, he won't complain to the gendarmes anymore if he drinks this."

Chick-Chick took the mug and brought it there, nearly falling down on the way, but she merely tripped, spilling only a small amount of the liquid.

"Uncle, uncle, Mári Chaba s-ssent me, you won't complain to the chendarmes anymore if you drink thish."

The old weaver looked at the little girl in horror, his face growing pale.

"Is there poison in there, my child?"

"Mári Chaba ss-said you won't complain to the chendarmes anymore if you drink thish ..."

The old man groaned:

"I won't complain ... I don't even want to anymore ... God put that thought into Mári Zsaba's head: I've already complained enough, I won't ever complain again ..."

He took the mug and set it in a safe place.

"I'll drink it soon, my child, but I still have a little work to do, first I'll get the dung cleaned out."

After that he grew truly depressed; he went out back for the pitchfork and got on with his work. Chick-Chick stood around by him for a bit longer.

"How did you get so bloodied up?"

"Mári Chaba hit me over the head with the roshary and with her Szeged ss-slipper too."

"S ... ssss ... sss ...," the old man whispered to her.

"Sss ... sh-ss-sh-ss ... ssss," Chick-Chick answered him, and the s-sound came nice and clean from her lips: "sslipper ... sss ..."

The next day was the big laundry day. Already before dawn they prepared the warm water, and the child likewise had to crawl out from her covers.

"Come 'ere."

She had to go over, Mári Zsaba washed her head in the lye. This burned to the point of covering her scalp with sores. The woman just ripped the hair from her head by the roots, then cried:

"Oh how God is punishing me with this mangy, wretched curse of a girl."

The lye was terribly strong, the little girl screamed, she shut her eyes to protect them from the soapy foam. Mári Zsaba was still in a rage, the old man remained alive, nothing had changed, the entire world had it in for her, and she drove her fist so haplessly into the little crying machine's mouth that she shoved in two of her teeth.

Now the blood streamed from her mouth.

It's a wonder a person doesn't suffer a stroke over all this wretched, dreadful, beastly misery.

She had to tell the doctor that the cow had kicked the girl, that's how her teeth had gotten shoved in.

"What's your name, my child?"

"Awffaweena."

Mári Zsaba cast a hate-filled look at the little girl: the mere fact alone of a child's having a name like "Orphalina" was unbearable to her.

The doctor couldn't understand it either, someone had to explain it to him.

"She has no name, so they entered this idiocy on the papers, Orphalina or some such rot."

"Orphalina?" the doctor laughed, "that's sweet. She truly is a little Orphalina. Open your mouth now, little orphan child ..."

And he gave her an injection and straightened something in her mouth. After that he gave her a kind of red medicine to wash her mouth with and rinse off her teeth. But the best medicine of all was that he always spoke so cheerfully and sweetly to her. He kept caressing her face with his soft, perfumed hands, and tugged at her tiny little button nose.

"All better, little orphan child, now just be sure to wash your mouth out well."

Right, but as they went home, Mári Zsaba took the red medicine away and used it herself, as it was just red mouthwash, and good for her as well.

But little Lispy protested:

"For me too!"

"You don't need it anymore. You don't need any more medicine."

She used it all up, the child didn't even rinse her teeth with it except for the one time.

"Shut up, or I'll punch your face in with it."

She hit, she beat, she bit, she did all such things, the hussy.

❀

The old uncle died two or three days after that.

The little girl knew what death was, she'd seen the one dead man, the ghost, Kadarcs, whom papa dear had shot. This time she dreaded the thought of seeing the old dead man, but she had to, because Mári Zsaba likewise feared going out to see him, even though there was one thing she was keen to know, namely what had become of the mug? She shouted at the little girl:

"Lispy ... go to the stable and get the mug."

"What mug?"

"What mug? The mug you brought to the old codger on Easter."

Aha, Chick-Chick knew now what mug she meant, and she ran off. Now she forgot about the dead man and only remembered the mug. When a person has a job to do, she isn't afraid.

When she entered the stable, the old man was lying there on the bench, as though he were merely sleeping; she didn't even look at him, she just looked for the mug, it wasn't there in the wall where old uncle had put it that evening, she had to look around again, and there if you please, she sees that the mug is back there beneath the dead man.

She runs into the house and says:

"The meg's there, the meg's there, old uncle's drinking from it."

She had to say it two or three times before Mári Zsaba understood her. Then the woman bellowed at her:

"Didn't I tell you to bring it over? Bring it here immediately."

So she had to amble back, but now how to retrieve it from off the bench. Old uncle couldn't hand it to her if he was dead.

She found the milking stool and placed it in front of the bench, stood on it, and reached into the bedding over across the old dead man. She grasped the mug, brought it forth, then got down from the bed, restored the milking stool to its place, then ran into the house and handed it to Mári Zsaba:

"Here's your mug."

But Mári Zsaba grew pale, she felt sick, she wanted to scream, but someone was in the kitchen, so she hurled the mug into the corner of the kitchen so that it broke into pieces.

"This ox drags every sort of dirt in here," she said.

The people were scandalized that they had the viaticum administered to him in the stable, although the weaver's house as well as the good border fields were left to them. But the people don't get it: it's imperative to accumulate property this way, there is no alternative but to resort to every possible means. Whoever devotes his life to this goal honors every tiny penny, takes it and sets it aside and never gives anyone anything. Accumulating property is a great burden and a great struggle. It requires an enormous capacity for shame. It's best if one has skin so tough that he doesn't notice when others find what he does improper: for he has been cleared of all wrong-doing, he is accumulating ... *Thrifty* is what they call him, and they expect nothing else of him. Neither gifts, nor alms, nor justice. The thrifty farmer promises the reapers three kilos of bacon, and while his father, who was not thrifty, gave five, he himself gives out only two kilos, with the excuse that it was three kilos with the basket included. The thrifty farmer says further: I plow your fields, and in return you work here for six days, until the corn silo has been filled. They work and they work, then he reveals that, as long as the silo hasn't been filled, all the work they do on the farmstead is unpaid. Nine days spent among the carrots, the corn, in the silo, and they still owe him three and a half days ... And how he has them work, the thrifty farmer; he says: So, people, this evening there are clouds in the sky, don't stop harvesting until everything is under cover, even if the dawn comes; but for this work, done during the night, the thrifty farmer doesn't pay a thing. At best they get a scolding if they don't work fast enough.

The thrifty farmer likewise knows well how to exploit the state child, he scolds little Chick-Chick to no avail, he asks for another state child from the lady of the manor, a little boy from Pest, "illegitimate here, illegitimate there," he'll make a good little swineherd. But Ferenc Szennyes is growing his wealth, his father was rich, and his wife, and the grandfathers were all rich, and all of them were wedded to fine, cheerful wives, as the life of the thrifty is very gloomy, however even the best man manages to turn a blind eye if his wife hoards a bit, he doesn't need to say a word to her about that. Who the hell cares if the dog barks, as long as it's a good watchdog. Nor does the finest man get his knickers in a twist over that, as long as he doesn't have to sully himself in the trivialities of economizing: just let the woman dirty herself – so his wife earned the chance to sleep peacefully in her bed while the little girl took the cow out before dawn, barefoot in the frost.

And he was oblivious to the fact that sometimes the little girl was overcome by ghost-induced terror.

Once on a cold winter's night the girl had to work watering the beasts – and when she looks up she sees a ghost in a white sheet, then when it nods, overwhelming fear courses through her, as she was alone and old uncle was already dead; she ran into the kitchen: a ghost, a ghost.

Inside there everyone shudders, as they were all of them uneducated, even the greatest wealth doesn't shield them from ignorance, and they rush out to be frightened by the ghost.

But they see nothing.

Little Chick-Chick took a few wallops.

One day when she was looking after the cow, she saw that the gendarmes were coming. She laughed, as the gendarmes had never caused her any harm, or maybe she was chuckling over the things they'd neglected to ask that day back then; she hid so that they wouldn't see her.

The gendarmes went to the farmstead, what were they doing there, what not, for a good while, then they left again; the little girl laughed to herself when they didn't even glance over at where she was.

At noon when she brought the cow back home, Mári Zsaba just says:

"I won't be bothering with you any more, you dog, I'm giving you back to the ones who foisted you on me."

"See – did the gendarmes ask why you don't send me to school?"

But Mári Zsaba didn't answer, she just looked at her from the corner of her eye. "They said that Dudás hanged himself."

Little Chick-Chick started to laugh.

"He was always saying he'd hang himself: I'll end you, I'll end you, together with myself."

But Mári Zsaba didn't reply to this either.

"You. Are you mad at me? Are you?"

"Yeah, I'm mad."

"Why?" And she cast a frightened look at the child.

"'Cause you beat my head with the rosary."

"Come, then, I'll make it all better."

All day long the woman snuck around, grumbling to herself. There was no understanding what she was after. She didn't say a word to anyone, she just spoke under her breath.

Orphalina went out to the yard, she dashed about like the little lamb and the chickens. She still lacked a sense of responsibility, didn't yet understand enough what her job was to do it of her own accord. "Get along! Don't!" she said, flailing at the ground with the switch. If they told her: do this, she did this, if they told her: do that, she did that, but it didn't occur to her on her own what she ought to be doing.

It struck her that it was nicer in the yard than inside the house.

The big mulberry tree had already begun to color its tiny fruits red, but nothing on it was edible yet. Nor was there any other fruit yet, only the currants in the garden were starting to turn red. But she could lay no claim to them. Why else, the currants have other business than to take a gander of little Lispy's belly: they're expected at the market, they barely succeed in ripening before they're whisked away. But the hens could care less about that, and the crested one snatches up at a dangling berry and plucks it.

She had to teach the creature a little discipline with the switch.

"Lispy!"

The little girl stood in front of the stable and looked in. She just stood there and looked. Sparrows were flying out of the stable, how outrageous of them to venture into someone else's stable. So she scolded them as she'd learned from others, the sparrows always deserve to be scolded, as the sparrow does zero good, it just pecks away the kernels left out for the poultry.

"Lispy!"

Orphalina was fully aware that the woman was calling her, but she didn't want to hear her, as bad things always resulted from that. Just let her yell, that's what Zsofka had taught her, who even said: "Just keep yelling until your throat splits." But she was just banking on its taking some time before the woman approached her and grabbed her girlish hair, until then there was no rush. She didn't act like she didn't hear anything, she acted like there was no rush in doing her bidding.

"Lispy, what the hell! Don't you hear me? May lightning strike you, how long are you gonna make me yell?"

That much she could understand, and when she sang this tune, it was time to make tracks and do her bidding, as: don't wait for me to come after you!

So she shambled over toward the house, with lowered head and her fingers in her pouty mouth.

"Come here now, my child," Mári Zsaba said, "how you look, my, you're just like an orphan child that nobody cares about."

Lispy peered up at the woman with half-closed eyes. There she stood, beaming corpulently in the sunlight, like a rosebush. But the rosebush is full of thorns, and Lispy was just waiting to see when the smack would follow this pleasant tone. But the woman removed the little yellow comb from her hair, sat down on the little bench in front of the house, which was located where flowers had bloomed, but the bed was empty now, as the flowers had been piled on the ground.

"Well, come here, then, come here, I'm not going to bite your ears off."

Ultimately she succeeded somehow in inducing the girl to approach her. The child moved toward her a little, too, she then reached out for her, thus she managed to pull her over to her, and she started combing her disheveled hair. She always cut the little girl's hair in a circle, parallel with the base of her ears, so it wasn't hard to comb. She didn't let her grow her hair out like the peasant girls. This didn't bother the little girl, she liked that she was somehow more special this way.

"Just tell me, you, what were you talking about with the old man that time, when you were coming back from church?"

The little girl didn't answer.

"Were you complaining about me? Just tell me. What was the old codger rattling on about, did he say we took his fields from him?"

The little girl nodded her head. She said yes, that's what he said, except she didn't know what that meant.

"So that's what he said. May he rot there, wherever he is. What else did he say? It's just lucky that he croaked, as he would have had it rough here staying with me ... Telling such things to a little girl who barely knows her own name ... What else did he say? Did he say he had a big house in the village? ... Did he? of course he did. And that I set it on fire, he said that too?"

The little girl shook her head, no, he didn't say that. He didn't say anything about setting it on fire.

"They set it on fire when there was war here, but that old wretch would just as soon have pinned that on me too. You see, no matter how good a person is, they're always wishing you harm. I took him in, the dastard, the crapper, I kept him here and washed his rotten, filthy shirts, his drawers, and then he tells such things to a little girl."

She pulled on the child's hair, as it was all matted together.

"So what else did he say? Why don't you tell me? Do you think I can divine your thoughts?"

"Nossing else."

"What do you mean, nossing else? When are you finally gonna learn how to talk? To hell with you and your mother too. That I should have to put up with someone else's brat when it had a mother of its own. It didn't enter this world in a bush or a piece of filth like a flea. But maybe that's you, a flea born in the dust, of the dust, that's what they say, you hatched that way, like a fungus. What business do such things have on this earth? So what else did he say? Did he say that I got rid of his wife, too?"

"I told him that papa dear alwaysh brought me to him, and he alwaysh ss-said not to tell mama dear he wash playing wich me."

"What did he do?"

Well the little girl had no idea what to say about what the old weaver had said to her, but she had a great deal to say regarding what papa dear, Dudás, had done with her.

At first Mári Zsaba listened wide-eyed, then she burst out laughing, and in the end she was so disgusted that she thrust the little girl away from her.

"Phooey, so now you're a disgusting slut. And no one told me that. Phooey, what a pig of a man that Dudás was, that's why he hanged himself. The gendarmes said he was suspected of some crime or other that had him frightened, but I thought he'd stolen or murdered or the like. Ough. He should have hanged you up with him, head down. Phooey, you pig. So little, yet so repulsive. Phooey."

She spat and spluttered, she couldn't go far enough to express her disgust.

After the little father's burial, Mári Zsaba was unrecognizable. She was so strange the entire summer long. But that was good, until then she hardly ever sat in the front room, but now she wasn't to be budged from there. At least they didn't see her.

It was all the same to Lispy. She just took the cows out to graze.

Summer came to an end.

"I have to go to ss-school now."

But Mári Zsaba didn't hear her, she paid no attention. Like someone who's always fretting about something else.

Once she says out of the blue:

"You told that to the gendarmes?"

Orphalina stares at her.

"I saw how they grilled you as well. Are you stupid? Don't you understand? On the road that day. Don't you remember? You were standing around there by the milestone, you were jabbering away to the gendarmes. So what did you tell them?"

She already knew, she remembered what Mári Zsaba was talking about, but it didn't matter to her; frost had formed outside over night, and she murmured bitterly to herself:

"I should be going to ss-school now."

Mári Zsaba shot a worried look at her:

"You've got a big mouth, but you still don't know how to talk. How to hurt others, that you know – I've got you pegged."

Suddenly she emitted a wicked laugh, grabbed the child and wrenched her toward her:

"Hey, you, did I ever do you wrong? you ...! 'Cause you got smacked once? ... Let's see your teeth, I even got them fixed for you, took you to the doctor, you … The dentist."

She drew her towards her, and the little girl allowed her, in patient bewilderment, to stroke her scabbed head with her fingers. She even picked at it with her fingernails, but not such that it hurt.

Abruptly the woman said, her voice utterly changed:

"It's not all right for you to be angry with me, because I have a child."

"But I don't have a mother, and your kid is legitimate."

Mári Zsaba began to cry.

"It's not all right for you to say bad things about me, child. If they ask you what's wrong with your head, you have to tell them you got scabies, that's where the scabs came from, but I cured you!"

"With lye."

"Not with lye, the washing heals. You have to tell them I healed you. Was I ever mean to you? Your own mother couldn't have been nicer to you."

She hugged her, kissed her, and cried.

She held the child's two small cheeks in her two hands, then her eyes hardened, and suddenly it looked like she would choke her.

But her arms and fingers only stiffened. Her tingling fingers froze on the girl's face, she twitched, but she didn't squeeze to the point of hurting her. In a word, she had no idea what to do with the girl.

After that she let the girl go again, Lispy could go where she wanted, and she went off, nonetheless hovering about once again, looking over her shoulder from time to time in the direction where she thought the woman might be. She, for her part, hurried across the yard as though she were looking for something or had forgotten something. She went all the way over to the kitchen garden gate, maybe she wanted to pick some plums and take them in to town, but instead she turned around and returned just as swiftly back into the house.

Lispy just watched her with furrowed brow. As though the woman were going berserk over her.

But the meal was now ready.

Zsofka stood in front of the house and began shouting.

"Hey, farmer sir, hey."

She listened. Indeed, the farmer was working there out back, behind the stable. He was digging something, his sleeves rolled up.

"Dinnner!"

Lispy saw from the fence how the farmer does indeed put down the shovel, shoving it into the dirt, then immediately turns, all flushed and sweaty – he wipes himself off and goes.

She rushed off as well, as she has to bring him water to wash with.

The table was set in the kitchen.

But Lispy took her meal on the doorstep. There she sat beside the dog, waiting for her plate.

Then suddenly the woman comes out from the kitchen and hands a mug to her.

"There."

Lispy wondered what's in it and looks: milk.

It made her wretch that they were giving her milk. She turned up her mouth, then merely held the mug.

The woman didn't bother looking at her, she merely said:

"There."

❀

The woman went then into the kitchen, and gave her husband his meal. When she came out, she didn't even look at the little girl, she went into the house, from there a child was heard crying. The little one in the cradle bawled and whimpered.

When the woman came out from there, she hadn't spared so much as a single word for her child; she went back inside the kitchen, but didn't cast a glance at Lispy. What did she care if I drink it or not, Lispy thought. Just handed her the milk: drink.

But she made sure not to consume the smallest bit of it, she just held it beneath her nose; the odor revolted her as never before.

A minute later the woman came out again, then went back inside to her child, from there she came out into the yard, but she didn't look this time either to see whether Lispy was drinking or not.

"What's this woman running around for like a tortured soul?" said the farmer there in the kitchen.

"She's looking for something," the servant girl said softly.

"She's looking for her mind, and she's not finding it," said the man.

As the woman came inside, she stood over the little girl.

"Have some, my child," she cajoled her, as though they wanted to pull a loose tooth, and suddenly she grabbed the little spoon that was in the cup and stirred the milk with it. "Come on now, have some."

Once again she went into the kitchen. She could be heard seating herself at the table, her chair creaking. Her plate clanked too, as did her spoon; and the man started talking.

"The flea beetles have eaten up the seed, we have to put out new. There's always something. Something's always eating what oughta be growing. That God should have nothing better to do than to create flea beetles."

Zsofka cajoled him with a laugh, but his wife did not.

"What are you looking at there with those dagger-eyes?"

But the woman said nothing, she went back out, here she was once again, the terrified little girl spilled some milk on her knee, but she didn't look at her, she went back into the room, as though she were frightened. She kept her head turned away and just walked past.

She was inside only briefly, but still managed to disturb her child, who began crying miserably.

But she didn't bother with him, she left him there without saying anything to him, she just left the room and entered the kitchen. In silence.

The child cried and cried. He cried loud and long.

Lispy felt badly for him, and slowly, along the wall, she snuck inside to him, as she wasn't allowed to go in near the child. So she went as always, skulking along the wall, she crept all the way to the cradle, like the beaten cat creeping up to the forbidden dish.

Now a good idea occurred to her. To Orphalina. She took her bread and dunked it in the milk so that she could use it to dribble the nice milk into the little one's mouth. For it was he who needed the milk, not her. Little babies absolutely love that.

But it took so long for her awkward little fingers to dip the bread into the milk and then drip the excess milk back into the mug that, the moment she held it out towards the little baby's mouth, Mári Zsaba entered, uttering a roar like an animal that's being speared to death.

"She's killing him, she's killing him!" she gasped and bellowed. "She's killing him!"

With her one hand she grabbed the child and hurled her so that she fell against the door; all the milk spilled across the floor, and the mug shattered. With her other hand she pulled her little baby out of the cradle and clutched him to her chest.

Only once she sensed that her own flesh and blood was stowed safely against her bosom did she go over to Orphalina on the floor to stomp her soul straight out of her body.

But then the farmer was there at the door, he didn't understand his wife, why she was just kicking and stomping on the little orphan. However if he didn't grab hold of his wife, her next kick might just stomp the life from the girl's body.

"What did she do?"

"She's killing him. She's killing him." That's all the woman screamed.

"What killing, for Christ's sake, anymore everyone's killing someone."

"She tried to dribble the milk in his mouth!"

"And that's how she's gonna kill him?"

"She tried to give him poison!" the woman roared, unable to control herself, she just snorted and spluttered over and over: "She tried to give him poison! That demon. Oh, let me strangle her, oh, this is my end! Oh, God alone was my protector in sending me in to prevent this murder."

"What are you rattling on about there," and he grabbed hold of his wife and shook her hard. "You've gone completely off the deep end."

The woman came to her senses somewhat, but she was overcome by such terrible panic that she shook over her entire body, like when a wagon clatters along and jolts every bone in a person's frame. They had to take the baby away from her and lay him in the cradle, as now he was wailing as though Satan himself were after him. The woman couldn't help him, she kept lunging at little Lispy, as she wanted to kill her. In the end the farmer pushed Orphalina out of the room, she fell in a heap there on the porch and lay crying on the ground, her insides aching and throbbing. He shut the door on his wife from inside.

He had to grapple with her at length until she calmed down somewhat in her exhaustion. She couldn't stop rattling on about poison, poison, and how they wanted to poison her child.

"Zsófi," the farmer told her as he came out toward evening, "take this wretch to the parish. Bring her back where she came from. It's clear to me that the woman will lose her mind if she lays eyes on her again. Take a ham to her: a shoulder. A shoulder will suit the gentlewoman fine, ha."

They laughed together.

That evening Orphalina was once again at the gentlewoman's home.

She looked around her in wonder. It was odd to her that she was already familiar with the odor that existed here and no place else. She knew everything. Not that she recognized everything singly that was here, it was all different from how it should be, but she understood the whole.

Here there is something great, something powerful, where they don't hurt her, its being here is good for her. And she began to trust in there being something good here.

Even her fear subsided, her pain abated. Rather somehow she felt inside like she belonged here. Here it was better for her than where she came from, where she was before, here something greater resided. She sensed security: she had only to turn to this place. She was still afraid, she feared that which was new, unaccustomed, but already she clung to it.

Felt secure in it.

If only she knew in what: she felt secure in this smell. She knew that, wherever she senses this smell, this nice smell, they won't beat her there.

"If you please, ma'am, she is a very sickly little girl, we can't use her," Zsofka said.

The lady of the manor looked with suspicion at the chubby servant girl.

"Why didn't the woman bring her. What's her name?"

"The woman? Mrs. Szennyes."

"Yes, yes, Mrs. Szennyes."

"She's ill ... since she had her child she's always sick. And her nerves are bad."

"Aha."

"She sent along a ham."

"Yes ... She's a good woman in any case ... Just put it here ... Well, it's no problem. There's a woman just now, Mrs. Verő, she wants a little girl. It will be good for her there, as she lives near the school, at least she'll be able to go to school more easily."

Chick-Chick was thunderstruck. The word frightened her: *Mrs. Verő – Mrs. Beater.* The name alone ... Where were they wanting to dump her again ... Once more she has to leave from this goodness ...

What kind of smell will there be there? ... a stick smell or a whip smell? ... Verő – Beater ...

The lady of the manor placed her white hand on the little girl's head:

"What's your name, then?"

The child peevishly pursed her lips. But then she muttered:

"Orphalina."

"Oh, yes, you're the little orphan ... Orphalina State ..."

She smiled pensively first at the girl, then at the ham.

"What's the matter with your head?"

The little orphan gave a sulky look, and slowly, after a length of time, she said:

"S-sscabies ... sss ..."

Seventh Psalm

The little girl looked around her crossly. She tried to look as though she didn't notice, but in her little heart she felt as though everything in the world were against her. She sensed something terribly wrong in the fact that, once again, they were sending her to a new father and a new mother who were neither father nor mother, and as the village draws closer and closer, they'll lock her up, too, like the pig when they want to fatten it, then they won't let her out in the field anymore, she'll have to stay home in the cramped pen, and when they finally give her corn to eat, they'll no longer let her out in the run, that's how a creature is dealt with who's destined for slaughter. God's beautiful holiday comes, Christmas, no one rescues the poor innocent from being pierced with a knife, like the little boy did to the little state child, from being brined ...

"Look here, Vater," the machinist's wife said, "I brought a little state child."

"Vater" was a big-bellied, fat, filthy person. He sat there in the kitchen eating salted bread. He looked sullenly at his wife, barely even glancing at the little girl:

"At twelve o'clock the woman's place is at home. You should have gotten dinner ready, but instead in this stinking house everything gets looked after except for my dinner."

But the wife paid no attention to the man, unlike mama dear, when papa dear – when he was still alive – used this same tone to quarrel with her. This tone was familiar to the little girl, though since then she hadn't heard this sort of family conversation, because Ferenc Szennyes was a completely different type, nonetheless that was how she learned that the family father usually spoke with the family mother, that was the proper way. She knew likewise what she had to do then: she quickly moved close to the door so that, if the need arose, she could escape, or if necessary, go for help.

Meanwhile her eye wandered round the room, seeking out what that genteel quality was that the manor lady had held out to her, no longer will you be among peasants, you'll be among educated people, and you'll go to school.

She saw this educated quality nowhere at all, the kitchen here was just a kitchen, at best the floor made a clomping noise when people walked on it. It was just as black as floors elsewhere, only gradually did she notice that the floor was made of planks, but it was neither scrubbed nor painted, it was just dirty. And the kitchen cabinet – that was actually like none she'd ever seen before. It was tall, and full of drawers arranged in two columns – maybe the educated quality the manor lady had promised her was in all those many drawers.

Mrs. Verő came and went, with fiendishly quick speech she told of what she'd discussed with the lady of the manor, who'd praised the girl to the skies, but she'd seen that she had lice or maybe scabies, her head was full of scabs, but she'd already made up her mind, Vater, that she was going to take in a state child, as there was so much work here, it would be good to have one, a state child needed little, and then you had someone you could send wherever there was a need, Vater.

Chick-Chick withdrew in mental retreat, it was clear to her that she wouldn't be going to school, once again nothing would come of that.

Now for the first time in her life she realized that she must also do something if she wanted to live. What, she didn't know, but some feeling hardened within her that she wouldn't put up with things. Nor did she know what it was that she wouldn't put up with, she merely thought she wouldn't let them just piss all over her. She'd allowed herself a little defiance in the past, but now she was ready to take that a step further.

She wanted to know where she was, and who these *educated* people were. This dirty, greasy, foul-smelling man whom the woman kept calling *Vater* wasn't too concerned about his wife, regardless of what she was saying, he just started chattering much more rapidly than she about his own stuff, mill this, and mill that. Nothing but the mill, the mill, all she knew about mills was that they numbered among those things, the mills did, that if they were mentioned, the peasants in the old places she'd been just bad-mouthed them. She felt all the more hostile toward these people if they were mill people, because she sided with her old foster parents in hating them, as they hated them so vehemently. Well that was a fine thing, to end up with millerfolk of all people. She covered her eyes with her two small hands, she didn't want to see the devils whom she'd always believed to be filthy black devils, and now they were her new parents.

The two people didn't bother much with her, they spoke simultaneously, paying little attention to each other. Chick-Chick didn't understand the adults' conversation terribly well, she only knew that the normal practice in conversing was to alternate, first the woman speaks, then the man speaks, but the two of them speaking simultaneously, that she hadn't tried yet. Maybe that was why they were speaking so quickly, like when a person grinds corn with his little hands, as long as kernels are beneath the stone, it goes slowly, you have to take firm hold of the handle, but if the grist runs out, then the millstone runs like crazy, even by itself: that's how their tongues flew.

"Well now, come 'ere, show yourself," the miller's wife said, "this is *Vater*!"

With this she grabbed her by the shoulders and perched her in front of the big-bellied man.

"You have to call him *Vater*. Do you understand? Say it, then, *Vater*."

Chick-Chick put up a little resistance. She said nothing, but she wanted nothing, she simply didn't know what the deuce this Vater was.

"Say it now, Vater, and me you call Mutter. Strangers call Vater Mr. machinist, and they address me as madam. But all you have to say is: Vater, Mutter."

The little girl understood one thing now: these were in fact not millerfolk if he was Mr. machinist. She knew that a Mr. machinist commanded respect, as she knew that when the wheat was being threshed it was important to cook something nice for Mr. machinist. Now she looked at the man and saw that he was indeed educated, as the ends of his moustache were trimmed off.

"Vater," she said slowly, timidly.

"So you see, we're your parents from now on. Yes?"

"Yes," the little girl said even more quietly, but in her mind she was turning over something entirely different: namely that now the wife was surely going to ask her from this point on to *love* them. But instead of saying that, she only said:

"So look, from now on you'll do whatever we tell you."

For two days they didn't tell her to do anything, and the little girl was telling herself, this isn't bad, this isn't bad, here all I have to do is play, nice, this Vater-Mutter-calling thing is pretty sweet.

But on Monday morning the Mutter said:

"Auf."

She had no idea what that meant, no one had ever come up to her and just said auf.

"Can't you hear? I said auf. Up out of the bed. Enough lying around, go and watch the pig."

Aha, that she knew all about, and she jumped up out of bed. But it was terribly cold, she'd been freezing all night long, too. During the night the kitchen cooled off but good, and these thin, tattered blankets offered absolutely no warmth.

Outside the sun was already shining, but the wind was blowing. She didn't even wash up, didn't comb out her hair; freezing, she walked out toward the pigsty like an aged servant who's neglected her duty. The Mutter just watched and saw that there was no need to say much to this one, she knew what she had to do. She opened the door to the pigpen, shoving the bolt to the side with a stone, as it was stuck, entered the sty, opening the interior door as well, and let the big fat pig out. The pig had an inordinately large belly, surely there were piglets in there, she recognized that with a single glance.

"Here piggy, piggy, piggy, come on out, damn it."

The Mutter just watched and laughed.

"Do you know where to take her? You can't bring her to the fields, since the wheat's sprouting, there's a penalty if she roots it up, but then too I'd tan your hide. You can only take her to eat along the roadside. Go out there along the field path, but be very careful that the pig doesn't damage anything."

She continued her lengthy lecture, but she didn't need to tell Chick-Chick any of that, as she knew all of that full well, she'd taken enough cows and pigs out to graze, she'd manage this big-bellied, black beast, too.

"Wait, take this scarf here and wear it, the wind's blowing."

Chick-Chick looked up. It had been a long time since she'd even heard of a parent caring that the wind was blowing.

She got an old gray scarf, but it was good for all that, the Mutter tied it around her at the back beneath her shoulders, and like a plump little two-legged bundle, she ran after the black pig.

She had no food along, but she figured that's how it had to be here, that was nothing new. But suddenly the Mutter comes walking along on her long legs and brings her something.

"Why did you leave your bread there? It was there ready for you on the cold oven, that was yours. I just noticed it when I was about to light the fire."

And once again a terrific flood of endless words just spills and spills from her, as ...

After that no one looked out on her until evening. The packet contained bread and cheese. Nice, generous portions. She was satisfied, she'd gotten more than was customary elsewhere, therefore these certainly weren't worse than her other parents. She began to sing, she was pleased to find a nice, pliable switch, with that she could guide the black pig beautifully, she needed that so she could monitor her along both sides of the road; the pig could root from beneath the acacias all the way to the sowed field, but she had then to keep to the inside, walking along the edge of the field, so the pig wouldn't trample it.

The wind stopped as well, and it looked like this was school for her. Until now she'd mostly grazed cows, and today she had to stroll alongside the black pig.

Her face was chapped from the wind, she had plenty to eat, at noon she ate the other half so she wouldn't have to carry the paper package anymore. She couldn't manage to chew the heel, so she tossed it to the pig, who gobbled it up with great enthusiasm.

But as dusk fell, the pig, as though someone had whispered in her ear, suddenly turned around and began galloping back home. She ran like the devil, it was all the girl could do to run after her.

When they reached the village, the Mutter was just then standing out on the street and saw them, how the pig was running ahead, the little girl behind her, shouting and throwing clumps of dirt after the animal to get her to stop. But the Mutter thought she was chasing the pig to make her run home faster, and she grew terribly angry.

"What are you doing to that pig, you wretch?"

The pig ran in through the gate and rushed straight into the sty.

The Mutter, for her part, took hold of the switch, tearing it from the child's hands, and struck her with it.

"Are you going to chase the pig again, you wretch? Don't you know that that pregnant sow will abort if it runs like that?"

The little girl stopped in her tracks and looked with terror into the towering woman's eyes – these two round, blue eyes flashed coldly at her, almost jumping out like two glass balls.

"Just wait, but I won't beat you with this, I don't want to leave welts on your body; I'll use the *Pracker*."

They went to the yard, and as they did the woman spoke without cease, offering such important lessons regarding swine hygiene as would have done an agricultural instructor proud. Finally she'd guided the little girl up to the house, and she went into the kitchen for the "Pracker."

Chick-Chick had no idea what that could be, she'd never heard that word in her life. Now she saw in the Mutter's hand something strange, a strange implement that was woven from slender twigs, its end shaped like a big dumpling. With this dumpling the Mutter laid into the girl and began beating her. The only comforting thing was that the welts on her weren't visible. The little girl was quite sensitive in this regard, she didn't like it when the welts were visible.

That's what resulted from all their education. Pig feeding beneath the trees.

The devil should take that pig, the girl thought to herself. For there was no other living thing in that yard. There there were neither hens, nor roosters, nor geese, nor ducks, nor dogs, nor cats, not even rats or mice. No pigeons flew down from the eaves, no swallows lived anywhere there, nor sparrows either, for what should a poor sparrow eat, should it go take its meals in the neighbor's yard? So if the devil took it and made off with that lousy black pregnant sow, then one could live in true peace and quiet at this house, maybe they'd even send her to the school so she wouldn't be in the way there at home.

"Mutter, when're you gonna ss-send me ta ss-school?"

"Oh, how frightfully you speak, like some kind of peasant. What kind of speech is that, when're you gonna send me to school? When, *if you please, will you enroll me in school?* That's how you need to speak. If you ask it that way, then I'll tell you when. After we slaughter the pig. Most likely the second term, you've already missed the first term anyhow.

"I'm always just miss-ssing it, miss-ssing it, miss-ssing it."

"Just look how she's learned to mouth off, with this atrocious language. Why do you say that three times, that you're miss-ssing it, miss-ssing it, miss-ssing it?"

But the little girl didn't answer, instead she took the pig out to forage along the road.

And she also learned how to drive her back home. She had to go in front, so the pig would follow along behind her. But she wasn't allowed to strike her on the snout, as otherwise she would abort, meaning she would lose her piglets. She had only to wave her hands around in front of her and hold her back that way. Yes, but the pig had already been so impatient that afternoon that such a small eight-year-old girl couldn't handle her. She broke away, once nearly biting the girl, and little Chick-Chick knew very well that, once a pig has bitten a child and tasted its flesh, then ten men can't tear the child from its teeth. At the Rudas's next door, that young boy who served as the neighbors' herder got eaten by their pigs. And he was already a youth of sixteen years. But when he beat the pigs to keep them from going where they weren't allowed, he fell among them, and the big boar bit him. It was impossible to save him. For that reason at noon she gave some of her bread to the black pig, who didn't even have a name, she was just "pig" – to get her used to her hand and arouse the pig's affection for her. In fact sometimes she received very little in the package she took along in the mornings, yet even so she gave at least a tidbit to the pig, as she was indeed fearful of this mad, gravid beast.

"Now the only place you can take her to eat is along the railroad," the Mutter said. "Take her out to the railroad, there the grass is nice and green along the embankment."

From then on, Chick-Chick went to the railroad with the black sow. The pig was already very large, and her belly reached to the ground. She jogged slowly along the long railroad tracks in the mornings, the girl loping along behind her: "Go, piggy, piggy, piggy, go."

Alongside the tracks the embankment was indeed a beautiful green, and the pig lived like a queen there, but the dastard soon noticed that in front of the storehouse there was always wheat or barley or some type of grain, meal, or feed that spilled out when they loaded the cars, and she immediately ran over there first of all if it occurred to her. But sometimes the pig forgot, it only entered her mind later, and then there was no stopping her, she dashed off to feast on the grain. Others also grazed their stock there on the grass, but none as much as she, since not everyone had a state child, and the mothers didn't have the heart to torture their children with grazing their animals there day in and day out, regardless of whether it rained or winter winds blew, and they didn't do it either, as a child can refuse to obey her mother, only a poor little state child can't.

Well, on this day, too, the pig suddenly raised her head at some noise or other, and began running between the rails toward the storehouse.

But the train whistled just then, and Chick-Chick was terrified that the train would run into the pig; she ran after her between the tracks with the switch and struck her so she would get away from there.

The engine driver saw that a pig and a child were running in front of him, but he couldn't stop the locomotive; he put on the brakes, and the engine screeched and hissed dreadfully.

The travelers who were standing there in front of the station all saw that in one more minute, just one more minute the child would meet her end. Their hair stood on end, they didn't even manage to scream, they were incapable of doing anything at that point.

The pig no longer wanted to graze, she only wanted to eat wheat, she didn't leave the tracks.

Then the train thrust them from the tracks and off to the side.

God knows how it happened, but both the child and the pig went sprawling off to the left on the ground in front of the station; by now everyone at the station was screaming, and they ran to see what had happened in front of the train as it rattled to a stop. "The little girl, the little girl!" they shouted, then it turned out that the little girl was lying in the dust, while the pig was already browsing, as she had already found some grain.

Nothing bad happened, except that the little girl was terribly frightened, that was it – the gendarmes came and wrote up an incident report, the women lifted the girl up and looked her over, even the engine driver got out, so that due to this incident the train spent a full three minutes at this little station.

"You didn't take a blow somewhere?"

"No, I'm just worried that I'll get it at home for this."

After that the train left, the travelers left, the gendarmes left too. For her part, Chick-Chick continued with the grazing; once the pig had consumed the grain she'd found, to the very last remnant, she went back to the embankment and continued grazing there.

That evening she then led the pig home. She went before her very cautiously, so that the miscreant wouldn't run off, nor was anything wrong with the pig, she didn't abort.

When she entered the yard, the Mutter looked out, but said nothing. Only once she'd locked the pig up in the pen and entered the kitchen did the trouble come. The moment she stepped inside she immediately received a terrible smack. After that a second followed, then came the Pracker, with that she got a thorough beating, even her little hands turned a solid blue, her legs turned blue and green, every blow was visible on her. Now it wasn't from whipping, but from heavy blows that she turned black. Beyond that, she was forced to kneel down on corn kernels and stay there for one hour, and on this day she was further punished by going without supper.

Little Chick-Chick cried and cried until she'd exhausted herself, she no longer even moaned, only the Mutter talked on and on about how she had to watch out for the pig.

But the little state child was carved of the kind of wood that made it impossible for her to be beaten to death. She survived even that, and experienced the great joy that something bad had, after all, happened to the pig, as the next day she didn't have to take her out to the railroad, moreover she didn't receive any admonishment or nice lessons with the Pracker, not even on the third day – perhaps the gendarmes had forbidden it, but the cause might also be that, several days later when they went out in the morning, the sow had already farrowed.

No one was with the pig, neither the machinist nor the machinist's wife. They understood nothing about their pig except how to talk about her a great deal, be it at night or in the daytime. The strikingly large-bellied pig had three piglets.

Chick-Chick laughed to herself, as she knew that she should by rights have had eleven. She didn't know why there were so few, but she said it was God's punishment for her having to run so much with the pig. Doubtless she'd eaten her young when she'd farrowed, since no one had been there with her.

The pig had it good for all that, as the machinist was a sort of miller after all, and of course they brought the feed home from the mill. She got so much that it was impossible to understand why they sent her out with the child to forage. Even in the pen they gave the pig enormous amounts of ground corn and grain, as well as water, and nothing else. They were fattening her. That was it, the pig ate and ate.

❀

It was already December, and Diti arrived from Pest.

This Diti was none other than the Mutter's own daughter. Chick-Chick soon learned that the Vater had nothing to do with the girl, he didn't even talk to her. The girl was in some sort of boarding school, she was something around twelve years old, a reasonably pretty, blonde girl, just extremely gangly. She was truly pampered, she got away with everything.

"Why are you keeping such a beastly state child, Mutti?"

That's what she said, and things became quite bad for Chick-Chick once she arrived. Not that she expressly hurt her, but she always said bad things, and she found everything that the child got excessive. Chick-Chick couldn't eat without her saying: "Why do you gorge that state child so? She doesn't pay for herself."

But Chick-Chick did nothing, she merely aimed an ugly stare at her. When Diti told on her for that, the Mutti came with the Pracker.

"Tomorrow St. Nicholas is coming!"

What could this St. Nicholas be? Here it seemed there was nothing but things the little girl had never heard of before. The bad thing, she thought to herself, was that there was always something else that resulted in her getting a beating. All parents beat the state child for different reasons. At Dudás's for this, at Szennyes's for that. Here for her bad pronunciation, albeit these Swabians didn't really even know how to speak Hungarian, they said such odd things and didn't even understand everything in Hungarian. Even their name was some newfangled name, they were the Schlägers, she'd heard that from someone in the street, a woman had said: those Schlägers will skin you alive, my child.

Here she was so useless. She always just loitered about. There was no work, she constantly had to sweep out the yard, even if a bird dropped so much as a ginger seed, the entire yard had to be swept.

"We'll soon see whether St. Nicholas cares for her, for the state child," Diti and her mother laughed.

"What could he like about that little beast? He has no use for a little beast like that."

"Baagh, beast," Chick-Chick said behind their back.

When she woke up in the morning, it was to the noise of loud screeching and laughter there in the front room. She who was in the cold kitchen couldn't imagine what was going on there in the pleasant warmth. For she always had to go in there when it was dark, while everyone was asleep, and make up the fire in the stove, but the moment it got burning, she had to leave the front room and sit about in the kitchen, or she could go out into the snow, that was allowed. But she wasn't allowed to stay indoors beside the warm stove, nor was she allowed to make up the kitchen fire before ten o'clock, because it wasn't needed for cooking. They had to save money. Here that was the operative word, from morning until evening all they did was save so they could prepare to leave the village – they were constantly talking about Pest.

"I'm not staying in the village," the Vater complained, "the pay is too low for me, there's no pension, and no contracts either."

But Chick-Chick thought to herself, damn it, what do you want. Every day there's meat, the Vater won't eat the food if there's no meat in it, and at every meal there's wine, half a liter for lunch, half a liter for dinner, indeed, that was her job too, the way to the tavern was very familiar to her, "just run and get a little wine, as Vater is coming for a drink." Yet it wasn't enough for them, the gluttons. Chick-Chick had not yet witnessed such good living, the Vater was simply unreasonable, for if something wasn't to his liking, he pushed the dish off the table, threw the paprika potatoes onto the floor if there was no kielbasa in them, or if lunch wasn't served promptly at twelve o'clock, then he didn't eat it. And now Diti's shoes were full of candy, as much as could be squeezed into them.

"Well, what's in yours then? What's in yours? Doesn't St. Nicholas like you? Phooey, you pig, why would he care for such a rotten state child. Bastard child. Who would give candy to her."

And Diti went haughtily into the front room, where it was warm, while the little bastard, the poor little state child pursed her tiny mouth, in an effort to keep from crying.

❀

But the Pátkay mill was actually famous. In fact Pátkay owned two mills. They said he spelled his name with a y, making him an aristocrat. Here every house belonged to the Pátkay mill, including the machinist's, the stoker's, the millers as well lived in his houses. Even his old parents were in such a little house, and this Pátkay was an expert at using his employees, for even the Verős received nothing but their meager wages. The rest they had to steal, as they didn't even receive a pig to raise, nor a garden, nothing. But one evening they came whispering, Vater Verő and a flour-covered man, who brought bran in sacks, these they poured out while careful not to utter a single loud word. They bought a few kilos of corn at the market, just enough so that the little girl could carry it home, but with this they could not have done much to fatten the big black pig after she farrowed; little Chick-Chick understood also why it had to be bought at the market, so they could discuss the price and how expensive it was, but by God! it cost nothing at all when the floury men poured a few half sacks into the bin. She'd never seen anything like this before, who could either father dear Dudás or uncle Ferke Szennyes have ever stolen from? Only from themselves. Dudás stole, but from his wife, in that without her knowledge he removed a sack of wheat here and there to the tavern with his wagon. And she herself had stolen a melon, for which they'd laid a hot ember on her fingertips, but no one had put coal on uncle Verő's, the Vater's fingertips during his childhood, as he knew very well how to direct where they needed to pour the grain, the meal, the flour, and everything they took.

The little girl was convinced that it was now her sacred duty to worry with the Mutter – oh, if things will just work out one more time ... oh, if only somehow they can avoid getting caught ... They even procured the coal this way that they used for heating. Particularly when Pátkay suffered a stroke, a mild one, then they didn't have to hide their efforts so carefully, they were able to take care of business quite well.

Thus Chick-Chick slowly settled into her role of constantly racking her brains to know what was lacking in the house and what needed to be pilfered from the mill. She felt at one with the parents in becoming a diehard and determined enemy of the owner.

But she took this so seriously that, even when she went to the neighbors to stand around and gawk, as children often do, she would not have spoken a single word for anything in the world regarding what she witnessed secretly in the dark.

The great grandparents were extremely old, in their nineties – the old parents of the mill owner. They loved her dearly, and they always had her sing and dance, and they gave her candy for it, and bread with jam as well.

"Oh, you little innocent," great-grandma said. "How is Józsi's little girl doing?"

Chick-Chick had just come from there, as the neighbor to the back was uncle Józsi, and he had a little baby in the cradle, a girl, who was always ailing.

"Sick," she said, "even her eyes are yellow, she's so sick."

"Oh, the poor innocent child," the ninety-year-old great grandmother muttered, "may God take her to him. It would be better if she died, for her and her parents too."

When Chick-Chick left them, she went right away to see the little invalid and learn whether she was still alive.

"What did the old folks say?"

"She said, may God take her to him, she's gonna die any way."

At this uncle Józsi began to cry, and he went over to the neighbor's, to the machinist's wife, and said my word, what mean-hearted people those old ninety-year-olds are, that they should wish death on a little baby.

Thus it came out that Chick-Chick had tattled.

Oh, what a ruckus that raised. It terrified the machinist couple that the little girl was a gossip.

When he came home, she told the Vater too, and he grew flushed. The greasy man turned as black as his clothes, and was as foul-smelling as witches' brew.

He didn't dare grab hold of the child, as he feared his hands would make sawdust of her.

But the Mutter said:

"Open your mouth."

Chick-Chick opened it, and the Mutter beat her mouth with a cooking spoon until it was full of blisters and so swollen that she couldn't eat for three days.

"Are you going to gossip again? Are you going to spread gossip?"

She roared at the child without cease. The Vater bellowed likewise, but with great restraint.

"Teach her, just teach her, the way her tongue flaps, she'll have even us entering the gossip circuit."

Chick-Chick screamed, then she realized they were afraid she'd blab about their nighttime hauls. That made her truly angry inside, as she could have told about those a hundred times already, but she didn't say anything, as she knew it was forbidden as a conversation topic. Now she shed heartfelt tears because these parents didn't grasp the loyalty with which she clung to them, and that she wouldn't utter a single word that could cause them trouble or harm, not for all the treasure in the world.

It shamed her, it affronted her most noble sentiments that her parents assumed she did not stand in solidarity with them in their thieving.

No, she'd never betrayed a thing, nevertheless after that she couldn't go along, couldn't even visit the great grandparents – she sorely regretted the loss of the daily bread and jam – and the Mutter even stood out on the street with her and cried out to the millerfolk to let them know that it was because of them that she beat the little girl.

"Oh, oh, oh," cried Chick-Chick as was her wont, as she had adopted the habit of starting to scream the minute they beat her, so that the neighbors would come running from all sides to see why the child was once again getting her hide tanned.

"Oh, if only I could die," she cried, but she couldn't even cry, as her mouth wouldn't move from its spot.

At such times dying would certainly have been best, for if her own mother had chopped off a piece of her, that wouldn't have hurt as badly, but when strangers did it, that was terribly painful, as she thought that her own mother would have smacked her differently from how strangers did.

"Get up, hold the basin."

She had to rush to her feet, this was the moment when the pig would be slaughtered, she had to go out, and she shuddered with dread, for it was true that she'd suffered a good deal over the pig, yet she didn't want to hold the basin when they slaughtered the poor thing.

It was all she could do to hold it, as she mourned so greatly for the pig. The poor thing was a very good soul – it would have been nothing at all for such a large beast to trample or even devour a little girl, yet she never did the child any harm, and she grunted so sweetly when Chick-Chick gave her some of her bread, and she let the girl scratch her neck, her big bristles, and when the sow lay down to rest as pigs generally did, the child could stretch out alongside her like she could by a cow, and the pig exposed her nice, fat, velvet belly and her four legs to the sky, then she could rub her across her thighs.

In the end she was just a poor woman, little Chick-Chick thought, she'd brought her children into the world and now her children were to become orphans like she herself, perhaps poor state orphans, they'll have a very tough time of it, they won't have their good, sweet mother anymore to comfort them in their pigs' language if their little bellies are hurting ... and she had only to hold the basin when they plunged the knife into her throat, because the Mutter had said she didn't want to see that, much less hold the basin herself ... and that wasn't a pleasant thing when the nice foamy, red, healthful blood spurted out, first splattering onto little Chick-Chick's clothes, but she wasn't afraid, instead she boldly pressed the basin up beneath the knife, and now the blood flowed nicely, streaming evenly into the vessel. "Stir," the slaughterman growled, "stir."

With a cooking spoon she stirred the blood as it flowed so it wouldn't curdle, but she only held the basin and stirred the blood because she was afraid to get beaten, as she knew they promised she would get it if she didn't stay in line. When she brought the blood in, they gave her dress a quick washing, as the warm blood that had splashed on it had penetrated to her undershirt, so she had to take that off too, and they gave her another shirt. How nice, Chick-Chick thought, that Rózsi, who'd worn her shirts, wasn't here – she could change clothes, since Diti didn't need the state shirt, plus she was big, too, bigger than her.

After that it was her job, once they'd done the gutting, to wash the intestines. To clean the foul-smelling excrement from the innards – she had to work just like the woman working beside her, but this didn't revolt her like the slaughtering did.

It was also up to her to stoke the fire, and because it was taking such a long time to clean out the guts, she constantly had to run over there, and the Szennyes's tub kept entering her mind: Chick-Chick, stoke the fire. She didn't even have time to breathe, she had work to do all the way until the dark of evening, for processing a pig is truly a big job. Of course the Vater wasn't at home, he only came at noon, when the freshly roasted porkchops with their lovely juice, and sour pickles alongside freshly pickled cabbage, were waiting for him.

"Is that all?" the machinist said. "Where's the pork broth?"

"That'll take awhile yet."

But this time the Vater didn't lose his temper, he was satisfied, for he said he loved the taste of the fresh meat.

"Well, whatever is lacking yet we'll get this evening at the slaughtering feast," he added.

The idea of the slaughtering feast put a bee in Chick-Chick's bonnet. She knew the term, but had never witnessed such an event, since at the farmstead they didn't hold a slaughtering feast. There they just killed and carved up the pigs, one after the other, but it wasn't the splendid sort of jamboree that it was in the village.

"Oh, how nice," she said cheerfully amidst her work, "I'll eat a slaughtering feast today."

But the machinist wife's daughter just laughed, she couldn't help herself. She teased her without cease about how she would eat the slaughtering feast. And she said it as though there would be nothing in it for her.

When dusk fell, the machinist said:

"Get wine."

She knew what that meant, as it was always she who had to go to the tavern. Whether it was to the store, to the shoemaker's, wherever, she always had to go along. Whenever Diti went to the store herself, her pockets were filled to bursting with candy, so she had to go with her. Diti ate the *szaloncukor* Christmas candies along the way, while Chick-Chick's mouth watered, but she didn't get any:

"What, you have no mother, and yet you want candy?"

Now she set out with the big demijohn, it was heavy even when empty, a ten-liter, round-bellied bottle. It was wrapped in wicker and had two handles so that it could be carried.

As she was going along the road, just going along, two people were standing in front of the apothecary, two strangers. It was a young couple, a young nobleman and a young noblewoman; she didn't know them, wouldn't even have looked at them, had the young man not spoken to her:

"Come over here, little girl."

Frightened, she stopped, but she didn't approach them.

Then the couple looked at her, and they took the initiative to go up to her.

"Tell us, little girl, have you got a mother?"

The little girl just looked at them without responding.

The young woman also spoke then:

"Just tell us, we mean no harm."

At this she said she had none.

The two grown-ups were shocked, they hadn't expected that.

"Why don't you have one?"

"I don't. Never did."

The strangers listened even harder.

"Orphan?"

"Not orphan. State."

"What?"

"I don't know, that's just what they say."

They stared at her in amazement.

They didn't know what this "state" could be.

"And where do you live?"

"At home."

"If you have no mother, whose child are you? A stepmother's, right?"

"No."

"Then who?"

"I don't know. The ones who beat me."

They were horrified at this. They found such guilelessness amazing – they didn't dare laugh, as the little girl with the strikingly large bottle in the windy cold of evening presented a truly frightful and sorrowful sight.

"Why do they beat you? Just tell us something about yourself. Look, here are twenty fillérs to buy candy with, just talk."

The little girl took the money, she was glad for it. She started to laugh.

"Just wait dear, I have candy, too," the pretty young lady said; she opened her satchel, took out two pieces of candy and gave them to her.

Orphalina took them, quickly piling them both inside her mouth at once. Hurriedly, like a cat that pounces when she gets food so that no one can take it from her. Just shove it in.

"So tell us now, as I've never heard of such a thing. Who looks after you?"

"I don't know. The manor lady from the league."

"Aha. The league. That would be the Children's League that the collection boxes on the street belong to. They usually collect money. Basically, you belong to that."

But the little girl just shrugged her shoulders, she didn't understand this.

"Miller. Mr. machinist."

"Who?"

"The Vater. Now I'm with him. I'm heading to the tavern for wine. There's gonna be a slaughtering feast."

She chattered enough to allow the young man to paint a coherent picture, which he explained then to the lady in the hat. He thought that perhaps the machinist had requested the little girl and adopted her.

"Is there absolutely no news from your parents?"

Orphalina just shook her head.

"Your mother doesn't come to visit you?"

At this she shook her head again.

"You've never seen her?"

Again she responded with a shake of her head.

A blush spread across the young woman's face. Who knows what was going through her mind.

What was going through her mind was whether the little girl's mama wasn't stopping to visit like this in the village, only to bring about the child's suffering ...

The young man took the big bottle from her and carried it himself.

"How will you carry this home when it's full?" the beautiful lady asked with concern.

Orphalina winked up at her. There was so much worry and kindness in her voice that it amazed her.

"Have you got a little orphan child, too?"

At this the woman as well as the man were briefly struck speechless, then the man smiled, while the woman cried out loud:

"Oh, my God," she shouted. "Oh, my God!" she shouted.

They were already in front of the tavern when the young man put the bottle down on the front step, and he went after the lady, who was running as fast as she could. But he looked back once, and when he saw that the little orphan was standing there, following them with her eyes, he gave her a five pengő piece.

"Here."

He wanted to go, but first he stroked the little girl's face, and said:

"Don't lose it."

With that he went after the young woman, and they disappeared in the darkness; it was impossible to see where they went.

Chick-Chick went into the tavern for the wine.

Fortunately the tavern wasn't far, it was nearly across the street from them, from their house, and the mill was there above them, guarding them with its great raised fingers.

"Well here's that beast at last," they said inside the house, "imagine if you let death wait on you like that. Where in the hell were you all this time?"

But it was all the little girl could do to catch her breath, after all it was hard to carry those ten liters of wine back home, so she laughed in lieu of a response.

"Go to bed then."

"I'm not going."

"What do you mean, you're not going?"

"Well I brought the wine, can't I eat the slaughtering feast?"

"Fine then, stay, the devil take you."

This made the little girl very happy, she started dancing and singing too.

"Maybe she drank some wine?" they laughed at her, as the house was full of guests.

"She's such a fool," Mrs. Verő said dismissively, and her daughter said with a pout:

"But mama, why do you let her stay in here. She should be in the kitchen."

"Let her watch for a bit."

This made the little girl happy too, that Mutter Verő didn't send her into the kitchen, but rather put up with her in here.

The Mutter packed a porcelain plate full of chitterlings and sausage, she stuffed so much onto it that Chick-Chick burst out laughing when she saw it. It wasn't possible to eat so much.

But she couldn't grasp the plate because the five-pengő piece was still in her hand.

She gave it to the Mutter.

"What's this? Where did you steal this from?"

And she began to raise a huge din:

"Look at this, this derelict stole five pengős in the tavern, then she hands it to me. Will you take it back?"

And she smacked her across the head.

"Hold off, madam machinist, ask her where she got it from."

"Where could she have gotten it from. She's a thief, she steals everything. That God should punish me with her. Where did you steal it?"

"I didn't st-st-steal it ... the lady gave it."

"What lady. What the devil. What sort of lady?"

"In the street."

"What street. Talk, or I'll stomp out your insides. There's no end to the bother you cause me."

"As long as the bother's no worse," a red-haired man laughed, "than a magpie's bringing home a little money. I had a magpie once, she brought me home a white-backed bill. Back in the day when the bills were white on the back. She was the only one who liked the money that was white on the back."

Everyone laughed. But the machinist's wife was keen to affirm that she wasn't one to raise thieves.

After that Chick-Chick slowly came out with what happened and how.

The woman didn't get it, but she didn't take the plate back from the girl:

"Tomorrow I'll sort everything out. Sit down, eat."

Chick-Chick sat on the little stool in the corner, nibbled at her food and watched the slaughtering feast.

She enjoyed it very much, and she was also pleased, as she sensed that they believed her words, and she wouldn't take a beating over the big, white, round coin.

The important thing was that she ate her fill and was no longer hungry.

At first the people did nothing, they just ate and talked about how nice the pig had been and how they'd only slaughtered her because she'd had piglets and they'd all croaked underneath her.

"It's not worth keeping something that can't even raise its own young!"

"No, no, madam," a fat, red-faced man laughed. "The piglets croaked because you kept beating the girl over the pig!" And as though he'd told some great joke, he roared with laughter.

The little girl in the corner there laughed too, and every time she thought of how the ruddy-faced man said that, she laughed, and she bit off another piece of the pig's gut, as though wanting to get satisfaction for all the beatings she'd taken because of the sow.

At some point Mrs. Verő cleared the table, leaving only the glasses on the tablecloth, filled with wine. Then they took to singing, crooning forth all sorts of old melodies. Then the butcher who'd slaughtered the pig, as he'd been invited too, began to sing: "In Budapest, in Budapest, the girls are roguish imps. Beneath their skirts, beneath their skirts, they love to show their limbs."

"Oh, please, don't sing that kind of thing – otherwise Chick-Chick will be caterwauling that tomorrow morning."

But whether they liked it or not, the little girl picked up the tune and, when they sang it a second time, she too crooned along in the corner: In Budapest, in Budapest, the girls are roguish imps.

After that it wasn't long before the guests went home to go to sleep; the Verős likewise started getting undressed, they prodded the girl: go to hell, you night owl – she's always poking her nose into everything.

During the night she dreamed that her mother appeared. She was large, strong, plump, but nonetheless identical with the beautiful lady that evening whose husband had given her money. Her mother told her she was taking her with her, but she didn't want to go, so her mother got out a rope and tied her with it to take her along. At this she grew terribly afraid, and she woke up, cowering with dread in the dark.

The next morning the word was that a young couple had been found at the edge of the woods, having committed suicide beneath some shrubs. When they were found, they were both already dead.

Orphalina also went out where the people headed to see the spot, but all she saw were the clothes of the suicides, and she realized that she'd spoken with them the previous evening, they'd given her the five pengős.

But she would just have liked to be able to see her mother one more time, and she knew that the young woman hadn't been the one she'd seen in her dream, as she was a small, slender woman, yet her mother was big and strong, and when she'd tied her hands it didn't hurt. But then she didn't know why she'd woken up.

When she looked at Diti, she said to her: "You see, I have a mama too, and she was just with me here in my dream, and she wanted to take me with her, but I didn't go."

"What do you have?" and Diti laughed out loud. "Did you hear what this wretch has got, Mama?"

But it no longer bothered Chick-Chick that they called her a wretch, she went out into the yard and began to sing at the top of her lungs: "In Budapest, in Budapest, the girls are roguish imps."

"I told you she'd be singing that today," Mrs. Verő said. "That pig has such good ears that she has only to hear a song once and then it's hers. It's a waste for me to get you piano lessons, you're as dumb as a gourd, I'm just throwing away the money."

"I have candy!" Diti said imperiously, and she called to the girl to go with her. She only took her along to show the whole village that she was eating candy along the entire way, without giving any to the one who was trailing along behind her, and Chick-Chick kept looking up at her like the dog at her master, her mouth hung open while dangling her tongue.

At that point the little girl saw there in the dust of the road a half-eaten apple core. She quickly picked it up, wiped off the dirt, and ate it with relish.

"Phooey," Diti said. "You're even lower than the lowest dog." She went home and told her mother what that ragged dog had done, and that she would no longer go with her as long as she devoured what even the dog left behind.

"She has no mother," Mutter Verő said.

"Yes I do," Orphalina thought to herself. "But if she comes here one more time, I'll leave with her too, I won't be staying here with you. Plus you don't even send me to school."

Now that she'd seen her, she thought more and more of her mother. Why does she have no mother if her mother's there? Why doesn't she come for her? Why doesn't she take her away? No one had ever seen her, but mama dear had said once that she was some kind of a noblewoman. And she'd also said she was big and plump.

"Come for me, kind, sweet mother," she cried to herself whenever she managed to hide in some corner or other, "take me with you, I won't be afraid anymore, 'cause a mother is allowed to tie her child's hands, and it doesn't hurt."

Nor would it have bothered her if she hit her with a Pracker, that wouldn't hurt either.

"I see now, I've had all kinds of mothers, with more to come, only my real mother isn't there."

Another time when she was hurting and raving by herself, she scolded her mother with the kinds of words that were used to scold her: "You wretched dog, you, why did you leave me here, dear sweet mother, why don't you find your little girl, get a rope, tie me and take me with you, 'cause my entire life I could never call anyone mother, and I could never lay my head on anyone's lap. When we went out to the graves of the dead, everyone had a grave except me, but I still lit a candle for my mother, I just didn't have a place to put it, 'cause my mama has no grave, even though I saw that you're beautiful, you're strong, and you're plump, and you wanted to take me with you. And now I have a candle hidden too, and I have matches, and I'll light it for you, Mama. I really will."

And she held her two little hands as though she were holding a candle in them, and the candle's tiny flame just flickered and fluttered in the breeze, like at the cemetery when she'd gone out there with mama dear and the many children.

But she no longer has her papa dear, nor Mrs. Szennyes either, since one day Mutter Verő came home and said during dinner:

"Did you ever hear such a thing, the gendarmes are looking for our little state child."

And indeed they were looking for her, the gendarmes took her off and questioned her about how the old uncle had died, the weaver, in the stable, and she told them that Mári Zsaba had given her the little mug to take to the old codger, and he'd said:

"'Is there poison in there?' 'cause Mári Chaba ss-said, he won't complain ta anyone anymore if he drinkss-s thiss-ss."

She was talking worse than usual, but she told it the same as back then.

The gendarmes understood her just fine, and after that the news came that they'd dug uncle up from his grave, and the doctors examined him, and Mári Zsaba was going to be hanged.

Then Christmas came.

Diti said that the baby Jesus brought the Christmas tree just for her.

Orphalina had never seen a Christmas tree, and she would dearly love to see it. Diti said that the baby Jesus would bring yet more presents, he'd bring them for everyone, for everyone, just not for the ones who were truly nasty, mangy, and evil.

Orphalina had to haul home from the market a big fir tree that they bought for money. Mrs. Verő had provided the money, and the child alone bore the tree, no one even helped her, but she wasn't allowed to drag it along the ground, so she had to carry it in her arms, but my how it pricked, the devil take it, its needles were so prickly that there was no good way to grab hold of it, it even pricked straight through her clothes. But Orphalina was the sort of child who, once she started something, she was bound to finish it. It would never have occurred to her to throw it down, even though she didn't even know what this tree was for, no one had told her that it would become the beautiful, famous Christmas tree. She actually believed the baby Jesus brought the tree, so if they'd told her what this tree was for, it wouldn't have made any sense to her.

For two days the tree was in the little shed in front of the cellar. This shed was built of wood, and all manner of things were heaped up in there. At one point they'd had a sheep at this house, its wool also lay stored here. And there was moss, and seagrass, which they wanted to stuff the mattresses with. Here little Orphalina dearly loved to hide, as no one looked for her here. And here her little candle was also hidden for her that she had to light for her mother.

She'd just sat down then when she'd come with the tree and had to put it in here, so that strangers wouldn't see it. That's what the Mutter had said.

Oh how awful it was before the holiday, she was constantly having to go to the market and haul things, and in the house there was all the roasting, cooking, all sorts of work. Her hands were eaten up by lye from all the washing. She had to polish the wooden dishes from morning until night with scouring sand.

But that didn't matter, the little girl was as though transported: tonight the baby Jesus would come, and he would bring the presents.

No one had ever brought her any presents yet, but the sweet baby Jesus was better than others. Her mother doubtless knew him too, as he, too, lived somehow in dreams. She'd met him at Easter when he lay wounded in a shimmering cloak in a majestic, shimmering casket beside the altar, but at Christmastime he was tiny and sweet. She trusted in him.

When night fell, the machinist came and said:

"Hey! ... Here's the ten-liter demijohn along with the one-and-a-half-liter bottle. *Lauf*. But don't go to the tavern. Go get wine from the peasant. Here's the money. You know where from. Andrássy Street. The guests are coming right away. Hurry. Run like the wind."

The little girl was somewhat afraid, since it was already dark, and the peasant lived very far away. Whenever they bought a lot of wine, five liters, sometimes on Sundays, then she had to go there. They put the two big bottles in a basket, and finally she was on her way.

It was dark, the moon wasn't shining, nor were there any stars in the sky, there was no light at all in the village. The only places that had electricity were the mill and the machinist's house, they got it from the mill. So when she went out from the bright light into the darkness, she couldn't imagine how she would get to the wine farmer's. When she left through the gate, the basket with the empty bottles was so heavy that it tipped in her hands, and it struck the acacia tree along the path. She was terrified that, if the bottles broke, it would be the end of her.

The machinist was watching after her and saw what happened. He quickly went to her and asked whether the bottles had broken.

"Uh-uh."

But he took them out and examined them – he saw nothing wrong with them.

"So just go, you know where."

"I don't know, how should I know."

"The hell with you, you stinking brat, haven't you been there often enough for brandy? But watch out for the bottles, because if you knock them again and they break, then don't come home, I don't advise it. He's there at the end of the village, where the road goes to Kecskemét, there's no other house there, you'll find it. It's not that dark."

"Go yourself," the little girl mumbled, but so quietly that the Vater wouldn't hear it.

And he didn't hear it either, he went inside, it wasn't for her sake that he'd stood at the gate, he'd been on the look-out for the guests – were they coming? No one came yet, so he no longer saw the point in freezing outside without his cap.

The little girl put the basket down, crossed herself, then lifted it back up and set off in the direction of Kecskemét. She had to follow Andrássy Street, if she would have known who this andrashy was, but she figured it wasn't someone who was out on the street after wine. She didn't encounter a single soul, only the acacia trees. She ran into two of these, as they were positioned so badly that a poor little state child who's out to fetch wine in the dark always bumps into them if her eyes are playing tricks on her.

Well, finally she got there, she didn't know that the dogs were running loose, she went straight to the porch, then two big dogs with a chip on their shoulder, bigger than she, came running toward her, and the one knocked her over along with the basket of bottles, causing her to start screaming. The farmer immediately looked out when he heard the barking, and yelled "Hey you, Csiba!" He shooed them off from afar, they weren't even biting, although the one grabbed the shoe on her foot and tugged on it.

"Ow, my foot hurts," the little girl cried.

"It's still all there," the farmer said. He measured out the wine for her, then accompanied the child to the gate. All he asked was: "Where're you takin' the wine?"

"To the Verős."

"So you're all by your lonesome? Can you handle those big bottles? They seem heavy for you."

Chick-Chick answered bravely: "I can handle 'em."

"Well, you're a good little girl. So be careful ya don't fall down in the dark. It'll be a nice Christmas for ya."

"Have a nice evening," the little girl said, and she took the basket's handles in her hands and valiantly set off with it.

It was true, the basket weighed down by the eleven and a half liters of wine was indeed heavy, she had to set it down each minute, she rotated it, switched it between her hands, even tried to hold the basket's handles with both hands, when a man spoke to her from above: "Where to, where to, little girl?"

Chick-Chick realized it was the farmer who lived next to the back of their house, and she greeted him cheerfully, saying good evening, uncle Móra.

"Is it you, you little sprout? What're you carrying there?"

"Wine."

"Wine? Here, hand it to me. I'll help you." He took it and said: "It's really heavy, you ... Is this your Christmas?"

The little girl huffed and puffed a bit, and began jogging alongside the uncle. In this way she avoided bumping into any acacia trees on the way back, instead running blithely along. When they reached the gate, the uncle put the basket down and said: "Don't say I helped you, my child, or you'll get beat up again by those Schlägers. It's enough if you say that you're all done in."

She opened the little gate wide, carried the basket in, but it was so heavy that she had to set it down and rest twice between the gate and the door.

"You're already here, then?"

"I'm here."

"It's a miracle that you're here."

But she just looked happily at him. She dared not say that she'd love to know whether the baby Jesus had already been here, because she thought she'd get in trouble, she just said nothing and looked around, wondering if he was coming.

All of a sudden, Mutter Verő said get out, I don't want you here.

She had to go out to the yard, and there she had to stand around in the dark.

She grew very sad, and the wind was blowing, too. Slowly she opened the door to the little shed and went inside out of the wind. There she looked for the little candle, she lit it and prayed to her mother:

"Mother, tell me that the baby Jesus is sending me some nice presents, 'cause there's no one to give me any, since I'm just a little state child, and the basket was heavy, even though a nice man helped me carry it."

She could think of nothing else to say, she just watched the little candle's flame as it burned, and it flickered and flickered, just like at the cemetery, where the wind had made it flicker.

She was here for a good while, and it was already getting very cold, she was freezing, then she heard someone shout:

"Hey, where are you? Hey."

She quickly left the shed and rushed into the kitchen, and left her mother's grave candle burning, as they were calling her.

"Why don't you answer! How often do I have to shout for you."

She didn't respond, she just went inside.

"Now you can have your dinner and go to bed."

But this shocked and frightened her.

"The baby Jesus hasn't even visited me yet."

Diti heard that and burst out laughing.

"The baby Jesus coming to such a mangy wretch. Jesus was already here, he brought me two pretty dresses, a pretty pair of shoes, a coat, three pairs of panties plus ribbons and lots of candy, even more than St. Nicholas. Oh, how little St. Nicholas does. The baby Jesus is the real thing. Topnotch."

"What did he bring me?"

"What would he bring to a mangy old state child!"

Little Orphalina grew disheartened. Then somebody opened the door, and a dazzling sight met her eyes from within. There in the middle of the table was a marvelous silver tree, all white and shimmering glory. And it was lit with electric candles, since the machinist had strung it with electric lights, as they got the electricity for free.

"What are you gaping at, you ass, haven't you ever seen anything like that?"

Orphalina began to cry, and said:

"No, I haven't."

Everyone started laughing at that and how stupid it was.

But without knowing how she dared it, she went then into the room without being asked, and stood crying in front of the tree, sensing only that she would never get to have something like this.

"Get out of here, you're not allowed to cry under the Christmas tree," the Mutter said. "Get out, go to bed."

"But I'd like to wait for the good baby Jesus to bring me something too."

"The baby Jesus was already here, he didn't bring you anything."

"You don't have a mother, go to hell, don't bother us," Diti shouted at her. And once again she started boasting about all the things she'd gotten.

But Chick-Chick didn't hear her amidst her crying.

At that point the Mutter took a piece of candy from the tree.

"Here, look, the baby Jesus sent this for you."

At this the little girl's heart filled with gratitude, and she didn't hear how they were laughing at her. She was utterly relieved and even began to feel happy that the baby Jesus had brought her something, too.

"Now get out and go to the yard, go around the well three times, then come back. Then your wish will come true."

Orphalina wished that her mother would come for her, and take her off into the great light, into heaven.

But they'd sent her out because they were expecting the guests, and the table had already been laid, and lots of dishes and silverware lay spread there. Now they piled it high with pastries, cakes, and everything else – they hadn't wanted for her to be underfoot.

Orphalina obeyed them, she went out, circled the well three times, then went back into the house. She believed that her mother would appear by now in the great light, and she saw how the eaves of the house were just blazing and sparking like a true Christmas tree, it was even sparkling. But it didn't occur to her that this was a fire; she just had to go inside, she thought, so that's what she did.

By this time the entire roof was burning. The shed was engulfed in flames, and there in the house the little girl wanted to tell them that there was an enormous light out on the house. But they yelled at her that she shouldn't say such nonsense. They thought she was just running her mouth because she'd dreamt something under the stars.

During the night the snow began to fall. The black Christmas turned into a beautiful white Christmas.

Three days later the burning beams had all gone out, and a thick layer of snow covered the remains.

Not a trace was visible that here a house had stood, and that people had lived there, and these people perished beneath the snow. Their voices perished, and their actions, the meanness perished and the cruelty. Everything grew peaceful, transformed, all of life took on a different nature. Their tongues turned to ash, their insults became vapor and smoke.

The end.

ABOUT THE TRANSLATOR

Virginia L. Lewis earned her doctorate in Modern German Literature in 1989 from the University of Pennsylvania and has studied various languages including French, Bulgarian, and of course Hungarian. She has written numerous articles on the literature of Germany, Austria, Switzerland, Romania, and Hungary. Her first translation of a novel by Zsigmond Móricz appeared with Library Cat Publishing in 2014 as *Gold in the Mud: A Hungarian Peasant Novel*. Dr. Lewis currently serves as Professor of German at Northern State University in Aberdeen, South Dakota.